A
PLAGUE OF
SORCERERS

A
PLAGUE OF
SORCERERS

MARY FRANCES
ZAMBRENO

Jane Yolen Books

Harcourt Brace Jovanovich, Publishers

San Diego   New York   London

Copyright © 1991 by Mary Frances Zambreno
Illustration copyright © 1991 by Greg Tucker

The first two chapters of this novel are based on
"Skinning a Wizard," a short story by Mary Frances Zambreno
first published in *Things That Go Bump in the Night*,
Harper & Row (1989), edited by Jane Yolen and Martin H. Greenberg.

Library of Congress Cataloging-in-Publication Data
Zambreno, Mary Frances. 1954–
A plague of sorcerers/by Mary Frances Zambreno.—1st ed.
p.   cm.
"Jane Yolen books."
Summary: When a magic plague begins to take its toll of
the wizards in the Empire, Jermyn, a newly apprenticed wizard,
and Delia, his skunk familiar, must find a way to stop it.
ISBN 0-15-262430-9
[1. Wizards—Fiction.   2. Magic—Fiction.]   I. Title.
PZ7.Z2545P1   1991
[Fic]—dc20   91-4419

Illustration by Greg Tucker
Designed by Camilla Filancia
Printed in the United States of America
First edition   A B C D E

For my mother,
ELVIRA ZAMBRENO,
who taught me how to dream,
and who never doubted.

And with special thanks to
DELIA DUTY, ANDREW SIGEL,
and ROBERT GARCIA,
who each contributed materially
to the existence of this book.

CONTENTS

vii

A
Plague of
Sorcerers

1

S KINNING A W IZARD

Y OU WILL accompany me to Weather Master
Fulke's because you are my apprentice, Jerry," Merovice Graves said firmly to her nephew, flicking imaginary dust off the top of the counter in front of her.
"I'll need you to work the crystal. Those maps in the
Weather Hall are good enough, but if we have trouble
locating a growing area, I want to be able to look at
it in the glass."

"I can't be your apprentice, Aunt," Jermyn said,
a little desperately. "I don't have a familiar. Yet."

The argument had been going on for hours. Days. Years. Jermyn pushed a lock of brown hair out of his eyes and regarded his aunt helplessly. A small woman, dainty in her best skirt and striped petticoat, she stood in the front room of her little herb shop and glared right back at him.

"And whose fault is that, may I ask?" she said, her mouth pursed in annoyance. "Rising sixteen the boy is, and not so much as a cat's whisker in sight. If only you'd *try*—"

Jermyn closed his eyes, counted to ten, and opened them. A wizard needed an animal familiar to channel power through, to draw mystic strength from the natural world. Apprentice wizards began their training the day after their inborn talent attracted a familiar. So far, it hadn't happened to Jermyn, and he was beginning to be afraid that it never would. Even Pol, Merovice's own great orange tabby, despised him. And what would he *do*, if he couldn't be a wizard? If he didn't have the talent to call a familiar to him? Hastily, he tried to banish the thought.

"I *have* tried," he said. "There isn't a cat on the dockside I haven't looked at, not a litter born I haven't visited. It just hasn't happened!"

"Then try harder," she snapped at him. "In the meanwhile, there's no reason you can't—"

"Aunt Merovice, please!" His own vehemence startled him as much as it startled his aunt. "I *will*

2

keep trying, but I can't pretend. Please, just let me stay home today."

"No." The single syllable made him writhe inside. "You have to face it, Jerry, lad. We've no reason to delay your apprenticeship further, familiar or none. There have been wizards without familiars—"

"Hedgewitches," he said. He didn't want that. He wanted to be a real wizard, a Guild member like Merovice.

"Mostly, yes, but still wizards, still magic-workers." Sighing, she picked up her cloak and bonnet. "You are my nephew, my own bone and blood. I raised you, I love you, and I know what's best for you. Trust me—apprentice."

"Yes, Aunt," he said, sighing. He'd lost again. As usual.

"Jerry?"

Something in her voice made him look away. "Yes, Aunt?"

"You *do* want to be a wizard, don't you? Really, truly?"

"Aunt Merry!" He stopped in the act of pulling on his cloak and tried to pull his astonished chin back into place. "You know I do. All my life—it's all I've ever dreamed of being."

"Well, if that's so," she said fussily, not looking at him, "if you're sure it isn't something I've just led you into—"

Jermyn put as much sincerity into his voice as he could manage. "I'm sure. Certain. Positive. I—I don't know why I haven't called a familiar yet, but I know it isn't for lack of *wanting* one."

She turned to face him. Her black eyes examined him, top to toe, as if she were meeting him for the first time. As if he weren't the orphaned nephew she'd raised from a baby but someone else entirely. He swallowed, and looked at the floor.

"I'm sure," he said again, low-voiced. "I just— don't know if I *can*."

There—his secret fear was out. But Merovice didn't seem surprised to hear it. She put her hand under his chin and forced him to look her in the eye.

"You do have the talent, Jermyn," she said quietly. "Didn't you learn to work my crystal when you were only seven, and years too young?"

Yes, and after years of practice I still work it with all the skill of a clumsy seven-year-old, he thought bitterly. "I know, Aunt. It's just—sometimes I get so tired of waiting."

She held his gaze for a few moments longer, then nodded once, decisively, as if satisfied at what she saw in his eyes.

"Of course you do," she said, and briskly turned away. "And no wonder. Let's walk, Jerry—the Weather Hall's not far, and Fulke will have a fit if we're late. *He* can be late, mind—but *we* can't. Ah, well."

4

"He's going to have a fit anyway when he sees me," Jermyn predicted gloomily, glad to change the subject. "He knows I'm not a proper apprentice."

"And why should he—well, and so he might." She cocked her head consideringly. "Small good it will do him. You may as well carry the crystal, since you're going to use it."

"Yes, Aunt."

He stood beside her, the little leather bag with the crystal wrapped inside it slung carefully over his shoulder, while she pulled down the door shade and then locked the front door. The gilt lettering on the big central window said only "M. Graves, Herbalist"; Merovice had never needed to advertise that she was a Guild master.

There was a soft *meow* from the windowsill. Pol wanted attention. He fluffed his orange tail out behind him and stared at his mistress thoughtfully.

"Now, Pol," Merovice scolded her cat indulgently, "we're off to the Weather Master's, and you know perfectly well that you can't come. Think I didn't see you last time, with owl feathers in your mouth? We'll have enough trouble with old blowhard Fulke arguing that the farmers need more rain than the woods can tolerate, without you making a meal out of his familiar. Yes, yes, I mean it—off with you."

The cat laid his ears back and blinked amber eyes already slitted against the late afternoon sun. Then he began washing a hind leg with quick, contemptuous strokes—whether because of Merovice's argument or the thought of Fulke's familiar, Jermyn couldn't guess.

The day was warm after an early shower, and Thornapple Lane was damp but bustling. Along its narrow, twisted length, craftsmen wove their way between shop and shop. Small children, dressed only in linen smocks, played tag running in and out of the ruts and corners.

"Nice weather," Jermyn commented, swinging into step beside his aunt. "Even for midsummer."

"It will be cloudy and cold again by evening," she predicted darkly. "Fulke couldn't hold sunshine like this if his beard depended on it, and that's not all. I don't honestly know what's wrong with the Weather Hall lately. We go from bone-cold to sunny in a single hour—why, a person could catch a chill and die of heat stroke all in the same day. Master Orthas would have had a fit. Now, *there* was a Weather Master. Bright, warm summer days, cool nights—and everything in season, mind."

"I know, I know," Jermyn said patiently. "Will we be out till evening?"

She shook out her cloak. "We may. Fulke would argue with the sunrise, given half a chance. Have Peter Quail and his gang of bullies been after you lately, by the way?"

"No—well, not much. Not since he was made

Fulke's journeyman." Hastily Jermyn changed the subject again. "Are we meeting Master Jodell at his shop?"

"No, he said he'd join us at the Weather Hall." Merovice stepped over a rutted puddle in the street and scowled as a passing pushcart sent a splash in the direction of her petticoat. "It will save him time."

The Weather Hall wasn't far from the Guild Hall proper, and some said that the weather wizards had the more impressive building. Where the Guild contented itself with soft yellow stone for its central house, its subordinate branch boasted a facade of white marble and intricately carved pillars, each one representing some aspect of the weather-ruling power. Merovice sniffed as they walked up the broad, shallow steps, averting her eyes from a pillar carved to resemble a woman pouring water out of an urn, representing Rain.

"Showy. Ah, well, weather wizards. They can't help it, I suppose."

Jermyn smiled absently as he pulled open the ornate bronze doors. Worked across the central panel was a relief of a bearded man bearing lightning bolts. "Is that why the Guild lets them get away with it?"

"It may be, at that," she said, stepping inside. She looked thoughtful. "Weather is power, the pure raw strength of the elements, but it has no fineness of touch at all. Remember that, boy. Power isn't everything."

"Yes, Aunt," he said automatically.

The entrance hall was also marble, a broad expanse of veined pink. The clerk at the front desk was a weedy little man with a yellow tunic worn over a stained linen shirt. His green eyeshade was pulled down over his forehead as he wrote busily in a ledger.

Merovice stepped up to him. "Merovice Graves, to see the Weather Master," she announced. "We're expected."

"I don't recall—let me see." The man made a great show of checking a list. "Oh, here it is. Follow me, please, Mistress Graves. Everything's ready for you inside."

She snorted and said to Jermyn in an audible aside, "I doubt it. I've known Fulke since his apprentice days, and he's never been on time for anything in his life. He likes to keep people waiting."

The clerk looked shocked even under his eyeshade, and Jermyn had to hold back a smile.

"As always, voicing your thoughts to all who might hear, Merovice?" Jodell said from the open door. Jermyn had always liked Master Jodell, Merovice's fellow herbalist and one of her closest friends. A large, comfortable man, he stroked his graying beard and smiled an absent greeting at Jermyn. "But you're quite right—Fulke isn't inside yet. That will give us a few moments to go over the figures one last time."

"Well, and that's kind of you, Jo," Merovice said.

"And at that, I've a few new words to say about next year's tansy crop."

"Not the wild mustard?"

"No—or not so much. Cultivated mustard works almost as well, and we've more than enough of that for most purposes."

The Weather Master's workroom was a large, airy place dominated by a tall arched window along the outer wall and filled with tables and desks. The clerk followed them into it, hovering nervously as the two herbalists placidly discussed technicalities. Merovice stripped off her cloak and handed it to Jermyn to hang next to the door with his own.

There was only one familiar in the room, Fulke's great snowy owl. Jermyn breathed a careful sigh of relief when he saw that Fulke's journeyman wasn't present; Peter must be on an errand.

Before Jermyn could join his aunt, the door to the inner office opened and out came Fulke. He was a big man, carrying too much weight for his size, with little pig eyes over a thin mouth and a pointed beard. He wore a rose pink court dress, which meant he'd been meeting with the Council of Wizards that morning. He looked almost insufferably pleased with himself.

"Quail, where's that volume of Ansemer's longitudinal declensions? I sent you for it almost ten minutes—oh." The Weather Master's gaze flicked over them. "I didn't realize we had clients."

"Your journeyman hasn't returned yet, Master,"

the clerk said obsequiously. "I believe these people have an appointment . . ."

"Of course, of course," Fulke broke in smoothly. His mustache curled with satisfaction. "The delegation for the herbalists. I'd almost forgotten—this morning's conference with the Regent ran rather long."

"The appointment was at your setting, sir," Jodell said, mildness itself.

"Yes, yes, I know. This way, Master Jodell." He had half turned away before he noticed that Merovice hadn't moved. Instead, she had settled back into her chair, with the air of one intending to sit awhile. "Ah, and Merovice, of course. You're looking well, dear lady."

She stood up, shaking her skirts as if to shake off the compliment at the same time. "I wish I could say the same for you, Fulke. I don't care what your tailor told you, rose pink is *not* your color. Not with your complexion."

Fulke lost a little of his satisfaction. "The fashions of Court demand—"

"Fashions of Court, is it!" Merovice's eyes widened. "And here I thought you'd gone color-blind in your old age. Are you working your new journeyman as hard as you did the last poor boy?"

"Discipline is necessary to a wizard," Fulke said stiffly.

"Discipline? It looked more like slaving to me,"

she said primly. The clerk darted a glance sideways at her and disappeared, as if he couldn't get out of the way fast enough.

"Now, Merry," Jodell rumbled soothingly.

Fulke's little eyes were cold. "If you'd chosen a field which required self-control, Merovice, you'd know better than to criticize others."

"Self-control, my left foot," Merovice snorted. "At least I don't rain all over the landscape when I'm in a temper. Besides, you know very well that we don't choose the field. It chooses us, when we make journeyman."

"Some fields are more difficult than others," Fulke said, smoothing his satin sleeve meaningfully.

"Yes, it's always harder to wade through mud than a clean street," Merovice agreed. "Oh, let's just get on with it, shall we? Jermyn, we'll need the crystal at the center of the map table, there. Set the base steady, and then key into it."

Even Jodell was surprised. "Jermyn's working the crystal?"

"Yes, of course. Why else would I bring him?" Merovice said. "He *is* my apprentice."

"Aunt Merry," Jermyn said uneasily, but it was no use.

"Apprentice?" Fulke said sharply. "He can't be. He doesn't have a familiar."

"He will, in good time," Merovice said, her chin

up. "And until then he is my apprentice because I say that he is."

Fulke looked annoyed. "Even you should know better than that, Merovice."

Jermyn tried to smooth matters over. "I apologize for the intrusion, Master Fulke, but I *can* work the crystal—"

He should have known better than to try. Merovice rounded on him fiercely. "Hush up, Jermyn. A wizard doesn't apologize."

"If you call this snirp a wizard, then your family has fallen further than I'd thought," Fulke retorted. "I've half a mind—"

"Obviously you have, you mold-eaten excuse for a sorcerer. If you'd ever had more than half a mind, you wouldn't try interfering between a master-class wizard and her apprentice."

Even Jodell was shocked at that. "Merovice, this isn't the time or place to quarrel."

"And what better place or time?" Merovice said, loudly. "Huh. Calls himself the Weather Master. Makes us wait like—like tradesmen! Insults my family—and just listen to that thunder! Temper, temper, Fulke! Who needs the self-control now?"

Fulke snarled at her. "Why, you—you hedge-witch! How dare you talk to me that way? I'm a member of Council—you can't—"

"I can do as I please!" Merovice snapped.

Jodell stepped in between the two. "Merry! That's enough. We're all Guild members—"

"Guild members!" Fulke raged. "Plant-grubbing herbalists—*faugh!* Continental magicians have more magic, and they spend half their time peering into the guts of dead animals. If I had my way—"

"You'd demote us all," Merovice snapped. "You've said so often enough. Well, I'm not standing for it anymore, Fulke. Do you hear?"

"*You're* not standing for—" Fulke swelled, momentarily speechless.

Jodell seized the moment. "Merovice, you can't mean to issue Formal Challenge. Not to the Weather Master!"

"I might," she sneered. "*If* I thought he had the courage to answer. How about it, Fulkey? Care to see what a 'mere herbalist' can do in a duel of magic?"

"You—you—" Fulke was almost hopping up and down. Outside the arched window, the sky had grown alarmingly dark. "You can't—"

Merovice sniffed. "I didn't think so," she said, and turned her back.

Fulke's roar made Jermyn wince; he could swear the walls rattled.

"Merovice Graves, you go too far! I'll see you fined for this! I'll see you in the stocks! I'll—"

"Ah, but will you answer my Challenge?" She sneered.

13

"You—you—"

It was too much. Fulke's response was not completely coherent, but it could have been heard by anyone in the building. In fact, Jermyn wondered privately if the Princess had heard it, all the way across the River.

"Good." Merovice nodded, when he finally stopped sputtering threats. "Standard three-day time span, no grievous physical harm to either person or property. Jodell, you'll witness for us that Challenge was issued and answered?"

"Certainly, Merovice," he said woodenly, but he was clearly worried. "What about the meeting we came here for?"

Merovice had the grace to look ashamed—briefly. "Well, I'll be resigning from the committee. Temporarily, of course."

"Of course," Jodell said, sighing. "Weather Master, if you'll excuse us, we will—"

"Go!" Fulke roared. "Get out of here! Now!"

They made it past the shaken clerk and out the front door before anyone spoke again, and then it was Jodell, who was at once anxious and irritated. "Merovice, how could you? You know how important the growing season is. Why do you *do* things like this?"

"It's all my fault," Jermyn said miserably. The light breeze lifted, turning colder as he spoke. "If I hadn't been there—"

Jodell hardly spared him a glance. "Your aunt would have found some other excuse for a quarrel. Haven't you figured that out by now? She and Fulke have been sparring partners since before you were born. I knew something like this would happen someday."

"Then you shouldn't be surprised that it *has* happened," Merovice said unarguably. She pulled her hood up over her head as they walked out into the open street. "There, see? Rain. I said the old blowhard was losing it."

"I just hope you haven't dug the hole too deep this time," Jodell said heavily. "Fulke's always been a dangerous enemy, but now—"

She sniffed. "Old blowhard," she repeated.

"Yes, he is, but he's also a weather wizard, with more raw power than you and I could dream of," Jodell pointed out reasonably. "If he loses control in a duel, he could kill you."

Jermyn went cold. "Aunt Merry, maybe you should—"

"Raw power isn't everything," she answered, ignoring her nephew. "A Challenge is a game of skill."

"There's also the fact that he's the Weather Master."

"What does that matter? I'm a master wizard my-self, you know."

"Master wizard, yes, but you don't rule an important and very independent branch of the Guild, and you don't sit on Council," Jodell pointed out. "Fulke could ruin you professionally if he put his mind to it."

She sniffed. "So? You heard what he said about my family."

"Yes, and I heard what you said about him! Merovice, face it. You've gone too far this time."

"I have not!" she said confidently. "Trust me, Jodell, I know what I'm doing. There are more ways than one to skin a wizard. Even a weather wizard."

"I sincerely hope so," Jodell said, and caught Jermyn's eye. "Your aunt always was headstrong, boy, but she seems to be getting worse in her old age. Take care of her, if you can."

"Of course he can," Merovice said. "He's my apprentice, isn't he? Come, Jermyn."

"Yes, Aunt." His heart in his boots, Jermyn followed.

2

DUEL OF MAGIC

MEROVICE'S PREPARATIONS for the duel were simple. First, she closed the shop, turning over the window placard and writing "Closed for the Holiday" on it.

"What holiday?" Jermyn protested.

"Should I write 'Closed to Fight Duel' on it, then?" she said. "No sense in frightening the customers. This will keep them away for a few days, and that's all that matters."

Traditionally, a duel of magic ran from sunset to sunset, with three full days between. As Challenged,

Fulke got first strike. He took it out in rain. A sharp crack of thunder rattled the windows in the rooms over the shop just as Merovice and Jermyn were sitting down to supper. Jermyn started and almost dropped his glass of milk, but Merovice only sniffed.

"About time." She went to the kitchen window and poked her head out. "It's raining cats and dogs, and means to keep up for a while. There's Fulke all over for you, never thinking of other people. He's got the storm focused right on Thornapple Lane. I don't know what the neighbors will say."

Jermyn's mouth was dry; he took a swallow of milk in a futile attempt to clear his throat. "What if Fulke loses control of the storm?"

She snorted. "He'd better not. Well, no sense in letting a good stew go to waste."

She sat down at the table and picked up her spoon with the air of one determined not to be disturbed by petty annoyances. They finished the meal in silence, except for the noise of the storm.

By morning, the rain had subsided to a light mist. Jermyn spent the day straightening the shelves in the front room, and warning away the few customers who ignored the "Closed" sign to knock hopefully on the door. Just at sunset, his aunt poked her nose in from the back.

"Still tidying up, Jerry? Why? It's neat enough."

She had been busy in the back room since early

morning. He didn't know what she was planning, but it seemed to take all of her attention and a good supply of the dried herbs that were the raw materials for most of her spells.

"I haven't much else to do," he pointed out now. "And I thought we might as well be orderly if Fulke is going to put us out of business."

"Oh, tosh, he'll do nothing of the kind. I've my protections set up now, and anything he sends us will just bounce right back at him. Tomorrow I'll—"

From the inner room there came a muffled *thud*. Merovice uttered a curse and a shriek which were not at all muffled, and disappeared into the back room. Closing the ledger, Jermyn followed her.

His aunt shoved a pallid, puddingy pot into his face.

"Look at this!" she demanded. "Just look! If the crucible hadn't given way, the whole tripod could have gone up."

Coughing, Jermyn batted away clouds of steam. "What—what happened?"

"The precipitate failed, that's what! How dare he? That—that *weasel!* I'll get him for this, by all the Powers, I swear I—"

"Aunt!" Jermyn said, firmly taking the ruined precipitate out of her hands and setting it safely on the floor. "What has Fulke done that's got you so upset?"

"He used a Great Magic, that's what he did! The

precipitate would have taken care of anything lesser."

"I don't understand," Jermyn said, confused. "What were you doing?"

"Use your wits, boy!" She glared at him sternly. "*Athame inferiori* is a protective spell—purely defensive. The fumes from it would have filled the air first in the shop and then farther around, and turned back whatever weathermagics Fulke sent this way. Haven't you noticed how the rain has been easing all day?"

"Yes, but I—never mind." He'd thought Fulke was just getting tired and letting the storm run its course, but he had no intention of admitting that now. "But if the athame-whatever-it-is worked—"

"*Inferiori*," she sniffed. "I should have used the *superiori* on him and sent him a plague of boils."

"Well, why didn't you?" he asked logically.

"Because I don't cheat!" she said angrily. "Didn't you hear me yesterday? No grievous damage to person or property, that's Guild law. And that's just what Fulke's gone and risked—there must have been lightning in that latest cloudburst. Well, I'm not going to put up with it!"

"You'll lodge a complaint with the Guild?"

She snorted. "And air my linen in front of the entire city? I will not."

"Well, but you have to do something, and fast," he argued. "Your defenses are ruined, and if Fulke is cheating—"

20

Her eyes narrowed. "You've a head on your shoulders, after all, Jerry—not that I ever doubted it. A quick response. Now, then, fetch my crystal."

"Aunt Merry—"

"Not a word. Go!"

He went. When he returned, she was sitting on the high stool at the worktable with Pol perched rather uncomfortably in her lap. He set the large cut crystal on the table in front of her—most wizards had such personal crystals, to transmit messages among themselves, and Merovice's was typical. Its diamond-shaped facets winked brightly against the dark wood of the table.

"*Tchah!*" she said, leaning forward to look into it. "I'm that upset, I can't concentrate. You do it, Jerry—I want to talk to Fulke."

Jermyn had enough magical sensitivity to work his aunt's crystal, but not easily. It required all his attention to feel his way delicately into the spiderweb network of energies, and even more to summon the image of the person he wanted to see. But in a few moments, the crystal misted over and the mist solidified into Fulke's ruddy, bearded face.

"Who calls?" Fulke asked abruptly. "Oh. You. What do you want, boy?"

"I'm the one who wants a word with you, Fulke," Merovice said briskly. "What do you mean by calling a Great Magic down on this house?"

"A Great Magic? Hah!" Fulke said. "I haven't done the half of what I could visit on you, if I wished."

"You had better not wish it, then," she retorted. "This is a duel by Guild rules, so witnessed."

He looked sly. "I'm not breaking any rules. You weren't hurt."

"You are on dangerous ground, Fulke," she warned. "If I went to the Guild with this—"

He smiled at her, his little eyes very mean. "What were you planning on entering as evidence? The wind?"

"I see," she said grimly. "So that's your game. My word against yours and weathermagics hardest of all to trace. Well, I won't play."

"What?" He looked confused.

"I've no mind to take this to the Guild," she said. "We can settle it between us, you and I. All I have to do is finish what you've begun."

His little eyes widened slightly. "You wouldn't dare."

"I will," she said. "I may not be able to summon a lightning storm out of thin air, but I can do a Great Magic or two of my own."

He scowled. "You're bluffing."

"Care to wager? Jermyn, break contact. Now!"

Caught off balance, Jermyn almost lost the crystal entirely when he reached back into it. He could hear

Fulke's roar of anger as he severed the bright connections and quickly shielded the whole.

"That's done it," he said, sighing. "I'll have a headache for a week, and so will he."

"Serves him right. You go take some camomile tea for your head, and put this away while you're about it."

She shoved the crystal at him. Surprised, he almost dropped it. "What are you going to do?"

She looked mischievous. "It's not we who are going to do anything, it's Fulke. He'll be worried, wondering—the magic of growing things is slow but powerful, laddie, and Fulke will be remembering that. He won't be able to wait for me to answer his lightning—he'll have to come see what I'm up to. And when he does, we'll be waiting for him. On your way, now, lad. We've preparations to make."

When Jermyn got back, she had the small saucepan out, with water boiling in it. Critically, she watched the bubbles and scattered a few flakes of some brownish powder across them.

"The spell's set in it already," she said calmly. "It's an herbal, not a Great Magic, but Fulke will never know what hit him. Breathe through your mouth."

"What? I don't—" The fumes caught him midword, and he gagged, wishing he'd taken her advice without asking: the essence of rotten eggs swirling through the room made him choke. Pol uttered a single, scandalized yowl, and vanished through the cat-door cut in the back wall.

"Pol!" Merovice cried, injured. "Well, I suppose I don't blame him, poor boy. A cat's nose is that sensitive. He'll be near if I need to reach him."

"What *is* it?" Jermyn gasped, his eyes streaming.

"For Fulke, of course. What he did to me stinks, and I want the world to know it. There are simpler magics than Great Ones, Jerry, and not a weather wizard living can work with his nose blocked up from a bad smell."

"I see." He didn't really, but it didn't feel like the right time to ask for an explanation.

"Good," she said. "Now, then, I'll need your help for this next bit—"

"Me? Aunt, I can't—" He fought down his sudden surge of alarm and forced himself to answer calmly. "What do you want me to do?"

"To start, move the long mirror over facing me. That's right, just tilt it so I can see the door in it from here."

They usually kept the full-length scrying mirror facing the door to the outer premises, in case a curious customer tried to peek in where he shouldn't. Jermyn wrestled the stand into a ninety-degree turn. It was heavy, and he got more than one lungful of stink by breathing incautiously as he worked.

"Is this all right?"

She glanced up. "Perfect. You stand to the left, facing it."

Jermyn did as he was told. "Now what?"

"I told you, now we wait." She sat back and crossed her hands in front of her. "It shouldn't be long until Fulke takes the bait. As soon as you see him in the mirror, I want you to hold his image in your mind exactly as you did when you called him in the crystal. It isn't cut, but the principle's the same. Can you do it?"

"I—I suppose so." A mirror was only another kind of glass, after all. "What good will that do?"

"It will keep him still—freeze him in place just long enough for me to get my concoction settled nicely onto him. An herbal takes time, but it is effective—you should be able to hold him long enough."

A thought occurred to him. He said slowly, "Aunt Merry, is this legal? My helping you, I mean."

She nodded her head. "Of course it is. Think I'd involve my own blood-kin in something that wasn't proper? You're my apprentice, and that means you can help this much and more. Besides, you live here, don't you? And Fulke will be entering without your permission or mine, which isn't proper at all."

"So I'd be within my rights to stop him and hold him for the Constabulary," Jermyn said, nodding back.

"You would. Not that it will come to that, of

course. When he realizes he can't get the odor off without my help, he'll pay the forfeit. Just don't be slow when he comes in."

"What if I am?"

She fixed him with a piercing eye. "Don't be."

The hours that followed were filled with tension. Jermyn and his aunt waited through twilight, past lamplighting, and into full night, crouched silently in the shadowed room. Every time Jermyn tried to say something, an admonitory hiss from his aunt held him still; every time she twitched, he jumped. Then, just as the moon was rising outside the workroom window, there was a noise like a hollow *thump* in the shop's outer premises. Jermyn started uncontrollably as the outer door opened and closed.

Merovice shook her head. "Through the front door. *Tchah!* Just like a weather wizard—no imagination."

The inner door opened slowly, and Jermyn stared at the shining silver expanse of the mirror.

"Aunt," he croaked, "he isn't there!"

"What? But he has to be!"

Something was there, all right. Jermyn could feel the hairs on the back of his neck prickle as the squeaky floorboard just left of the threshold creaked and went silent under an oddly familiar whisper of sound. *Oh, of course*, he thought.

26

"He's here, Aunt! He's—"

A flicker of light reached out at him from the emptiness by the doorway. Gasping, he threw himself sideways. His aunt's eyes darted about, searching for something she couldn't see. Wishing with all his heart for even a hint of real power, Jermyn fell against the crucible from the ruined defensive spell. With a desperate heave, he hurled its soggy contents straight at the source of the flickering light.

Head, shoulders, and hood of his cloak of invisibility outlined in sticky goo, the Weather Master stood in the doorway. Merovice cried out in relief, then started to giggle like a girl.

"An eyes-aside! Well *done*, Jermyn! Fulke, I didn't realize you were such a coward."

"A coward, am I," he said, a trifle thickly. "You—you—"

The weather wizard was right in front of the mirror, his face filled with rage. Jermyn could see the reflection move as Fulke started to strip off the soiled cape. His free hand was already raised, and before Jermyn could even think about fixing the image into the glass, Merovice tossed the contents of the small saucepan.

The potion caught the edge of the cape and spattered all over the floor. Jermyn goggled as Fulke shook out the cape to one side. It was too fast! She knew how slow he was with the crystal—why hadn't she given him more time?

Fulke sneered. "Is that the best you can do? Really, Merovice."

His hand reached out into empty air, opened and closed around a spell. Whatever it was, it couldn't be good: Merovice stood frozen.

"Remember this, Merry," Fulke said gloatingly. "Remember *me*—"

"No!" Jermyn cried incoherently, and flung himself between the weather wizard and his aunt.

There was a sudden hissing noise, and an odor even worse than that which had emanated from Merovice's saucepan filled the room. Jermyn's chest felt tight, as if he were going to explode. Hardly aware of what he was doing, he gestured with his right hand as he'd seen his aunt do a thousand times. Light streamed from his own fingers, and caught Fulke full in the body. The wizard cried out in shock and staggered backward—to fall directly into the suddenly smoky surface of the tall mirror behind him.

Jermyn stared. In seconds, even the image had dwindled into nothing. He licked his lips. "Where— where is he?"

"Gone back to where he came from this night, and good riddance to him," Merovice said. She was pale and clinging to the table, but her eyes were bright with joy. "You sent him through the mirror like a message into crystal—and he's taken a lovely smell away with him, too. Oh, my very dear boy, I always knew you could do it!"

"I don't understand. Where did he go? I didn't mean to hurt him—"

"You didn't," she said. For all her delight, she seemed almost uncertain—oddly off balance. "You just sent him home, all at once and using the mirror like the great glass it is. It isn't a common thing, and I doubt you could do it again for planning, but a surge of power is only to be expected in these circumstances."

"*What* circumstances?" he said, his voice rising. "What have I *done?*"

"Freed your own magic for use. Can't you feel it?"

Now that he thought, he did feel different. Sort of—lighter than air. "Where did the stink come from?"

"You called it out of the air, of course, when my own little plan went awry." She shook her head slightly, as if clearing it, and leaned backward onto the stool. "What is it—butyl mercaptan?"

"I don't know."

"Not know? Ah well," she said, lifting her right hand as she did to dissipate cooking odors, "best—get rid of it—before—"

For a moment, it seemed as though everything were back to normal. Then, stiffly, like a plaster doll, she toppled off the stool.

"Aunt Merry!" Jermyn caught at her frantically, and lowered her to the floor. She wasn't breathing!

Her heart—where was her heartbeat? He couldn't find a pulse.

For a long second he simply stared at her rigid body. Then he took a deep breath, placed his right hand over her heart, and *pushed*—with the new strength inside of him as well as with his hand. There was a ringing in his ears as his own heart clenched in pain; he ignored it and *pushed* again.

Merovice coughed weakly once, twice. Gasping, she batted his hand away. "What—what—Jerry?"

Limp with relief, he sat back on his heels. "You had a fit of some sort," he explained. "You stopped breathing. No, don't try to get up. Oh, all right, but not the stool. The chair's right here—"

She let him help her into the chair and then sat staring at him incredulously. "What d'you mean, I stopped breathing?"

"You did," he said. Shivering a little, he went to light the lamp. "Your heart stopped, too. I don't know how I got it started again."

"Never mind that now," she said, sounding almost angry. "What I want to know is, why did it stop?"

"I don't know that either," he told her, opening the window to let out some of the smell still thick in the room. "Could it be something Fulke did?"

"Before you blocked him, you mean? I don't see how, unless—" She stopped, and her eyes widened. "A curse. The weasel brought a curse with him! That must have been what he threw at me."

"A curse?" Jermyn asked, puzzled. "What sort of a curse?"

"It must be a full-scale curse on my ability to work magic," she said grimly. "That's the only thing that could stop me from invoking the Great Magic I threatened him with. Enough of it must have gotten through to take effect. Yes, and now I think, I was this minute pulling strength through Pol for a spell to get rid of what's left of this stink, and that must have triggered the reaction. Oh, I will *fry* him for this! I'll render him down to a salve for curing horse pimples and sell him to a diseased foreign merchant! I'll—"

"Why not complain about him to the Guild?" Jermyn said hopefully. "This certainly seems like intent to do permanent damage."

Almost visibly, Merovice controlled her anger. "It isn't that bad. And I will *not* make a public spectacle of myself. In any case"—she brightened—"he'll have to take the curse off, now he's lost the duel."

"What if he won't?" Jermyn said, worried. "What if he refuses?"

She shrugged. "We'll manage. Now, where's your new familiar?"

"My what?" It didn't seem right that she could sound unconcerned about something so important, but that was Merovice.

"Your *familiar*," she repeated, beginning to sound irritated. It also didn't seem fair of her to put her brush with death so quickly behind her, not when he was still shaking. "The beastie must be here somewhere, now you've called. I knew it would take some strong emotion to start you off. Your mother's family was all like that. They needed to *feel* things."

A sudden, dreadful suspicion gripped Jermyn. "My mother's family? Aunt Merovice, did you do this on purpose?"

"Did I do what on purpose?"

"Get into all this trouble with Fulke, of course."

"Me?" She was the picture of sweet innocence. "Why would I do that?"

"Because I was worried about not calling a familiar. Aunt Merry, if you *did*—"

"Really, Jermyn, don't be silly," she said, but she wasn't looking at him and he didn't believe her. "And anyway, it worked."

"Of all the unnecessary—you might have been killed!"

"Nonsense," she said. "The rush of power when a wizard first calls a familiar is more than enough to take care of any spell, even a Great Magic. I don't know how any part of the curse got past you, but—"

Jermyn ignored the interruption. "What if I hadn't been able to call? Or what if Fulke's cloak of invisibility had fooled us? It almost did."

"So there, that is a point." She looked thoughtful. "About the eyes-aside, I mean. I wasn't expecting that. Still and all, you handled it, didn't you? And it's finished, lad, so no sense complaining. Where's our new cat? I do hope he gets along with—"

There was a loud, protesting *meow* from the window. Pol stood on the sill, vibrating with pure feline fury.

"Pol!" Merovice said happily. "Pretty boy, I knew you'd be close."

Pol was in no mood to be cosseted. He hissed, glaring at the floor. Bewildered, Jermyn looked down. There, clumsily brushing up against his boots, was a flat, furry creature with a long bushy tail and a pointed nose. It looked a little like a black and white cat, but it wasn't. Automatically, he knelt and extended his hand to be sniffed.

"A skunk?" Merovice said, as outraged as her cat. "You can't have a *skunk* for a familiar!"

3

The Ideal Familiar

An afternoon not quite two months later, Jermyn was studying alone in his aunt's workroom when he saw his familiar start to struggle up onto the tripod holding the new crucible. He dropped the book and grabbed for her. "Delia! Get down from there! If you break that, Aunt Merry will have a *fit*—"

Her small, breathy voice answered him apologetically from the back of his mind. *Sorry, Je'm'n. Sorry-sorry.*

"Sorry won't help," he warned her, but he couldn't work up much of a scold; he knew she was only trying to get closer to him. And besides, not much *would* help between Merovice and Delia. His aunt objected to everything about his familiar. Even the name—

"Delia is a lady's name," she'd protested, on the morning after that momentous night. "You can't give it to a skunk!"

"I just did," he said, looking at the little skunk asleep in his lap. "Why are you so upset, Aunt? You've told me often enough that familiars don't *have* to be cats. Weather wizards always use birds."

"A familiar is always an animal with some dignity," she responded, glaring at the skunk. "A bird of prey, or a cat, or—not a skunk!"

Delia, rather unfortunately, had chosen that moment to demonstrate that she snored.

Jermyn had to smile, remembering, but Merovice's horror wasn't really amusing. Delia couldn't help being awkward and young and excitable, any more than she could help hating Pol—who hated her right back, with a spitting intensity that was very undignified in an experienced and middle-aged familiar.

Sorry, said the soft little-girl voice in his mind again, and he sighed.

"There now, it's all right—this time. You just go sit on your cushion and don't move."

The young skunk settled down contentedly in the corner on the big pillow—it was really more appropriate for a cat, being one of Pol's old ones, but Delia made the best of it. As long as she could watch Jermyn, she was fairly happy.

Go for walk? she asked now, hopefully.

"No, I am not going to take you for a walk," he said firmly, ignoring the thin autumn sunlight coming through the window. "I have to study."

Determined, he picked up the grimoire he had dropped when he'd seen Delia put her forepaws on the tripod, and tried to find his place on the page. *Oh, Powers! I might just as well start all over again.* He wasn't learning nearly fast enough. And he had to learn, because Aunt Merry was still carrying Fulke's curse.

At first she hadn't been worried, even though Fulke refused to remove the curse—refused even to admit that he'd lost the duel.

"Don't fret, Jerry," she'd advised him confidently. "We'll find the key to the spell, and when we do, you can remove it for me. You've the talent, you've a familiar to focus the power through—all you need is a little control."

But he couldn't seem to manage the power or the control, and they were running out of time. As long as Aunt Merry was cursed, she couldn't cast any spells, not even a standard preservative for the lotions and spices they sold over the counter. And until Jermyn learned to manage his new abilities, he was essentially useless in the shop. *Powers Below take Fulke anyway!* He almost had put them out of business after all.

Lost in his worries, Jermyn didn't notice Pol enter the room, but he was immediately made aware of the event. Pol announced his presence by leaping casually from chair to table—without disturbing so much as a leaf of the drying herbs waiting to be sorted—and then full on top of Delia, who, so far as Pol was concerned, was snoozing on *his* cushion.

Delia squealed in rage. Pol snarled, claws extended, and Jermyn grabbed for the broom. One swat separated cat and skunk, but the skunk's tail had already started to rise. Ominously, her forepaws settled onto the cushion but found no purchase. If she got to the floor and started to stamp and turn . . .

"Delia, no!" Jermyn shouted. He brought the broom down again, hard and fast. "Not in the house!"

The little skunk whimpered at him piteously—then scuttled off the cushion and, with a surprising turn of speed, scampered out the cat-door. Pol, his own tail inflated, made as if to pursue. Jermyn dropped the broom to reach for him and collected an armful of scratches and a torn shirt sleeve for his pains.

"You stupid cat, that is not your pillow anymore!" he fumed. "You've got a new one. Aunt Merry's told you and told you—why can't you let Delia have the mangy old thing?"

Pol hissed savagely, and Jermyn let him go. Well,

at least the cat had thought better of chasing Delia, but Jermyn had better go after her—fast—before she got them both into trouble. He grabbed his cloak and headed out the rear door of the shop.

There was a chill in the autumn air; he took a moment to shrug into his cloak. At least it wasn't still raining. No sign of Delia in the yard behind the shop, or in the lane beyond that. He stood still and concentrated. Poor Dee. She must be feeling terrible—he could sense her misery at the edges of his awareness like a thin red mist. But where?

Toward the river—of course. She almost always went towards the river when she was upset, running to hide under the big old hollow log by the riverbank. The tree must have been centuries old when it finally died; lying on its side the trunk was taller than a grown man. Delia had a burrow underneath it, probably a legacy from an old badger. When she backed into it, he couldn't reach her.

She was there, all right. Patiently Jermyn hunkered down by the aged wood and peered underneath it. "Delia? Deedee, are you there?"

No answer, but a soft, warm sigh disturbed the damp. "I'm not mad, honest. I didn't mean to hit you. I was aiming at Pol. He had no right to jump you like that."

This time he got a pair of bright eyes and the tip of a nose. Sighing himself, he settled cross-legged on the damp ground, leaned back against the tree, and stared at the river. The docks were their usual bustle. Jermyn could see the bright flags, hear the voices as workers loaded and unloaded cargo. He squinted: yes, that was a purple sail coming into port. The Princess Alexandra must have been out on the water today. It was said she loved to sail.

Delia? he called without speaking. *I love you, Dee-dee. You're my familiar—my very own special familiar. Please come out.*

A wet nose mushed itself cautiously into his hand. He took a deep breath and relaxed inside.

Sorry, Je'm'n, the repentant skunk said, her mind-voice even smaller than usual. *Sorry-sorry always.*

"Yes, you're always being sorry, aren't you?" he said, almost tenderly. Funny, the way a wizard could feel about a familiar. The little animals were necessary for working the stronger magics, of course; they provided the living focus by which a wizard pulled power out of the living world. He'd always known that affection was usually part of the link between wizard and familiar, but it hadn't been *real* to him until he'd attached a familiar of his own. "I'm sorry, too, honey. You can't help it. Usually."

He reached down and hauled her into his lap, where she settled with a contented little grunt.

Nice.

"What? Oh, the weather. Yes, it is a nice day. And you got your walk after all, I guess. Didn't you?"

A suspicion of a chuckle tickled his thoughts. Delia loved to be out-of-doors—the further and longer out of doors, the better.

I ought to take her out more, he thought guiltily. Of course, most familiars were quite capable of wandering around on their own, even in the city. Not Delia, though. She was too prone to accidents.

He leaned back again, enjoying the sunshine in spite of the chill. It really was a fine day, after all the rain they'd been having.

"Well, if it isn't the skunked apprentice!" a disagreeable voice said to his right. Jermyn tensed slightly, and Delia looked up at him worriedly.

"Hello, Peter," he said, taking rapid stock. Redheaded Peter Quail, Fulke's journeyman, was flanked by two of his cronies—not impossible odds, but not good. Carefully Jermyn set Delia on the ground and began to get to his feet as if that were what he had been about to do anyway.

"Journeyman Quail to you, Apprentice," the redhead said, sneering. He was still trying to grow a beard, Jermyn noticed, and it still looked as if rats had been chewing on the fringe. They were much of an age, he and Peter, and had been at Dame School together; their feud went back years, almost as many as Merovice's squabbles with Fulke.

Jermyn focused on dusting leaf mold off his pants. "If you wish, Journeyman," he drawled as insultingly as he could. Neither of the other two were journeymen yet, just senior apprentices. Even if they were currently attached to the Weather Hall, he could try to be polite to them. He had known them as long he'd known Peter. "Hello, Regis, Cassiday. What's up?"

"Not much, Jer'," Regis started to say. "We were just . . ."

A glare from Peter made him trail off in confusion.

"On an errand for *my* master," Peter said, self-importantly. "Council business."

Jermyn raised one eyebrow; Peter hated it when he did that. "All three of you? He must be slaving you, like Aunt Merry says."

Cassiday mumbled, "Oh, it's not so bad . . ."

Peter shushed him. "You wouldn't know about masters, would you?"

"I've got a master," Jermyn said, setting his teeth. "Merovice Graves is one of the most experienced apprentice-masters in the city."

Delia was crouched at his feet; a quick glance down showed her watching him closely. Maybe he ought to pick her up again—

Peter didn't give him time.

"Your Aunt Merovice!" he snorted. "Hah! The only thing poor little Merovice Graves is master of these days is her own kitchen!"

"Poor little Merovice! Why, you ignorant—"

Jermyn all but bit his tongue in an effort to hold back the words. As Fulke's journeyman, Peter would be aware of the feud and maybe even the curse, though the latter wasn't common knowledge. But if Fulke's journeyman and Merovice Graves's apprentice fought, it would be the apprentice who was in the wrong—the junior apprentice was *always* in the wrong.

"Why, Jerry!" Peter said, his eyes wide and oozing false sympathy. "Poor little Merovice has been having—trouble lately, hasn't she?"

A red haze obscured Jermyn's vision. It seemed as though he couldn't see anything but Peter's sneering face, and the compulsion to wipe that sneer off by rubbing the face in some honest harbor mud was so strong that it must have had sorcery behind it. Merovice had been a full wizard since she was fifteen, apprenticed at twelve. True, she'd never been on Council, but she was a master wizard . . . and *no one* called him Jerry but his aunt!

And then he heard Delia grunt, threateningly.

"Oh, no! Dee—"

"What the—" Peter pulled back, his face gone pasty white. "What's that foul beast up to? You can't—"

But it was too late; Delia had had a difficult day and her blood was up. Besides, a good familiar always knew what to do when her master was in danger.

"Gah!" As all three of his tormentors let loose

with identical disgusted cries at the sudden stench enveloping them, Jermyn closed his eyes and moaned.

It would have been funny if it hadn't been the fourth time this month—and if it hadn't meant another probable reprimand and fine. Jermyn trudged home with Delia tucked under one arm, trying not to despair.

Je'm'n mad? Delia asked, as much puzzled as apologetic. *Sorry Je'm'n mad. Whyfor?*

He repressed a sigh. "No, I'm not mad. You were only doing what you're supposed to do. If only—"

If only her attempts to protect him didn't have such wholesale consequences. A young feline familiar would have scratched and bitten and done some damage. But when Delia went into action, the aftereffect left two apprentices and one journeyman unfit for polite company and hence unable to work, which their masters wouldn't like at all.

At least Peter had suffered the brunt of the attack. Jermyn's lips quirked upward at the memory of his tormentor, eyes streaming, howling imprecations, stumbling down to the water in a vain attempt to wash himself clean. It would be days before Peter Quail was socially acceptable again, and it served him right, too.

The light was on in the back room when he cautiously let himself in and set Delia down on the floor:

Aunt Merovice was home. She was sitting at the worktable, industriously sorting herbs.

"Hello, Jerry," she said. Her nose twitched, and she lifted her head in sudden alarm at the faint odor. Delia never sprayed her master, even by accident, but she always left a trace.

He answered the unspoken question. "Yes, I'm afraid so. I ran into Peter Quail and his bullyboys down by the docks. Delia thought they were threatening me."

She flushed bright red. "Fulke's journeyman? Why, that—how dare he threaten you?"

"I didn't say they were threatening me, I said Delia thought they were," he corrected her, determined to get the worst of it out at once. "And from the way Peter reacted, I imagine that Fulke will lay a complaint against us. And Pol had another fight with Delia."

She looked down at her work. "I know. He told me."

Her back was resolutely turned to him, her attention on her hands. "If you'd just lend a hand here, lad," she said, her voice studiously innocent. "I want to get this lot tied up and hung to dry before supper."

"Yes, Aunt," Jermyn said automatically as he went to settle Delia on her cushion, but he frowned slightly. Such a quiet reaction wasn't like Merovice; what could be wrong?

He corrected himself as he took his place opposite her at the long table: what *else* could be wrong? For a while, neither of them said anything. Then Merovice broke the silence.

"Nephew, we have to talk."

"About what?" he asked apprehensively, stalling for time. When Merovice called him "nephew," it was serious. "Aunt Merry, if it's about Delia and Pol, I promise she won't bother him anymore."

She made a dismissing gesture. "It isn't that—well, it is, in a way, but that's only part of it."

"What, then?"

"You," she said bluntly. "When I left, you were reading Ordovicius, and that was the book I found open and waiting for you still when I got back. What did you do all afternoon? I expected you to be halfway through Responsions by this time. Did you do no work at all, or were you too busy dealing with that—that creature?"

"I did study," he protested. "I was trying to memorize the descant tables."

"Trying to memorize the tables?" For a moment, Merovice was distracted by her own bewilderment. "What for?"

"Well, I thought—"

"Tosh, lad, that's why we have grimoires. No wizard remembers everything. Unless you're some fool of a spellmaker trying to improvise at need—which I do not at all recommend, as it's a good way to get fried—you look things up in your spellbooks."

"I didn't realize," Jermyn said humbly. "I'm sorry. I tried . . ."

"You always try," she said. "Maybe that's the problem. You try too hard, and when the power comes, it—it overflows!"

Jermyn winced, remembering the last time he had tried to renew a preservative spell—refilling a jar of bath powder for Lady Destrain. The spell had exploded on him, sending a cloud of scented yellow dust swirling madly all over the shop, while the Lady herself had collapsed in a prolonged coughing fit. Lady Destrain was one of Merovice's oldest and most loyal customers, but she hadn't been back since.

"At first I thought it might be your creature," Merovice went on. "Seeing as how she isn't a typical familiar. It seemed likely she wasn't a strong enough focus for you—that you'd be better off with a new familiar—"

"I won't," he said quickly. "And anyway, it can't be done. Can it?"

"Oh, it can and all," Merovice assured him. "In fact, it's often easier the second time, once one has the way of it. If the first bonding was a mistake, the wizard only has to—banish his familiar and take a new one."

"But I didn't make a mistake!" he protested, and

hastily lowered his voice as Delia looked up. "None of this is *her* fault."

Merovice sighed again. "I knew you'd say that, and I think you're right. The bond is true. And besides, I never truly trust wizards who replace living familiars. And it isn't honest, somehow, to kill the poor little beasts."

"Kill her!" He swallowed a sudden huge lump in his throat. "Aunt Merry, I couldn't—I—I won't let anyone—"

"*Tchah!* Of course not, lad. I'm not suggesting you do. Besides," she went on as if she didn't hear his gasp of pure relief, "I said I thought it might be the beast's doing, but I was wrong. It isn't her fault—it's mine."

"Yours?" Jermyn gasped at the fresh shock. "What do you mean?"

"I mean you need a new teacher, Jermyn," she said soberly. "For I am doing you no good at all."

"But—Aunt Merry, you're the best 'prentice-master in the city!"

"I *was* the best 'prentice-master in the city," she said. "No longer. I didn't think it would be a problem, me being cursed, but it seems it is. Or could be it's even simpler than that. I was talking to my old friend Jodell today, and he reminded me that it never does to teach close blood-kin. That's why the Guild forbids a parent to instruct a child."

Jermyn felt numb. "But you aren't my parent. You're my aunt, and it's legal for an aunt to instruct a nephew."

Her face twitched unreadably. "You are as close to being my child as may be, Jerry. I hadn't thought— but there it is, and we have a problem."

"What do you want me to do?" he said, anxious and confused. "I don't *want* a new master."

She frowned. "That would be the usual answer. But when I asked Jo this afternoon if he could take you, he said he's full up, with three boys to bring along as it is, and he was that embarrassed—"

"Now, Aunt Merry, that's too much," Jermyn said, as firmly as he could. "Jodell's too easygoing to be embarrassed about anything, and you know it. Remember the time he was playing Wind-Foxer in the Spring Pageant and his costume pants split at the seams and he'd forgotten to put anything on underneath? Right in front of the Patriarch and the Mayor and the Powers Themselves, and all Jodell did was laugh!"

She gurgled, but choked off the chuckle sternly. "Oh, poor Jo—I'd forgotten that. All right, perhaps 'embarrassed' is not the right word, but he was not easy in mind, Jerry. The long and short of it is, there's no working wizard in Riverbend who doesn't know of this feud of mine with Fulke—"

"Our feud," he put in, and she nodded.

"Very well, our feud with Fulke. They can't know

how far it's gone—for once, the old blowhard has been as discreet as he should be—but they know that Fulke is the Weather Master and they want no part of a quarrel with him."

Jermyn took a deep breath. "And now we're in trouble with him again—because of Delia and me. Aunt Merry, what are we going to do?"

"We're going to eat dinner," she said, taking the last bundle of herbs from him. "That's first—it's roast chicken tonight. Lock up, will you?"

"Yes, but—"

"Pol! There you are, boy," she said, and swooped to pick up her familiar as he sauntered—ostentatiously innocent—into the room.

Jermyn plowed on. "Aunt Merry, if Fulke is Black Marking me, can't I complain to the Guild on my own behalf?"

"Not unless you want to get known as a trouble-maker and ruin your career before it starts," she said, standing in the stairwell with her cat in her arms. "Spellcaster Douglas is old and often absent from sessions, and Fulke won't let the Council listen to any complaints but his until he's good and ready. I should have known better, Jerry—Jodell said as much. I'm sorry."

"It wasn't your fault!" Jermyn protested. "All right, so you sort of started things, but it's Fulke who won't see reason since Delia scented him."

"Perhaps," she said, sighing. Then she smiled, impishly. "Ah, well, spilt cider is past praying for, and I've still a few tricks that the old blowhard won't expect."

"Aunt Merry," he started, alarmed.

"I hadn't thought it would finish like this," she mused, turning away from him to start up the stairs. "After all these years—but listening to Jodell this afternoon, I realized that the time had come."

"Aunt Merry, the last time you tried to trick Fulke—"

"It worked, didn't it?"

"Yes, but he got so angry he wouldn't take the curse off!"

"He always was a poor loser," she said. "Don't look at me like that, Jerry. I know what I'm doing."

"What?" Jermyn asked, even more apprehensively.

"We're going to go see an old friend of mine," she said cheerfully. "One who can help. Tomorrow, Jermyn my nephew, we visit the Theoretician—and Fulke can put *that* on his plate and eat it!"

4

THE THEORETICIAN

THE THEORETICIAN was named William Eschar, and he was that rarest of all creatures, a theoretical wizard. In order to make a living, most magicians focused on the practical aspects of their craft: the creating of things and the providing of services. A theoretical wizard dealt with the theory behind the magic, with the very laws of nature.

Jermyn had had no idea that Merovice knew any theoretician, let alone *the* Theoretician.

"No, he doesn't live in Riverbend," Merovice said crossly, struggling into her cloak the following morning. "He isn't an ordinary wizard, and there isn't anything of use to him down here. Besides, he has to be nearer Court."

"Why?" Jermyn asked, confused.

She snorted at him. "Sometimes I wonder if you live with your head in the sand! The leading theoretician in the Empire is always one of the Ruler's advisors. Or don't you remember your elementary civics? Not that I suppose the Princess will need much advice from Master Eschar until she comes of age, but he used to speak to her father quite often, I'm told."

"But he isn't a member of the Wizards' Council. I thought *they* were the Ruler's advisors on affairs of magic."

"That's your trouble," she interrupted. "You *don't* think. Now come along."

Meekly he followed her out the door. "Is he expecting us?"

"I doubt it."

"But—shouldn't you make an appointment? Most wizards—"

Her mouth set in a thin line. "*More* questions! I told you, Master Eschar is different."

There was no arguing with her in this mood. The day was overcast, but not cold. Jermyn thought wistfully of Delia as he and Merovice made their way through the empty morning streets. It would be a good day to go out along the river, but he doubted he would have a chance.

He cast a sidelong glance at his aunt's profile, and decided to risk another question. "Aunt Merry, why are you so sure that the Theoretician will see us?"

"He's an old friend." She hesitated. "And he owes me a favor."

That information so shocked Jermyn that he almost stopped dead in the street. The Theoretician was almost a legendary person, as much above an ordinary herbalist—even the best herbalist—as Merovice was above a common hedgewitch. How could she possibly have aided such a man?

His aunt didn't give him time to ask *that* question, even if he could have figured out how to phrase it safely. She moved so quickly that they were almost at their destination before he'd recovered enough to speak at all.

The Theoretician, it turned out, lived in Temple Square, which was one of the better quarters of town. Its wide stone streets were clean and swept, and no vendors walked down them. Over the walls that lined the roadway, Jermyn caught glimpses of tall, spreading trees—those would be in the central gardens he had read about, which must also contain the fountains he could hear splashing.

Merovice looked at him curiously. "You're gawking, lad. Haven't you ever been this way before?"

"Not that I remember," he answered honestly. "It's different."

"It'll be a new experience for you," she said bracingly. "Ah, here we are—Wisteria Street, second house on the left."

The gate in the white stone wall looked like any of the others: massive and wooden, with brass fittings. Calmly, Merovice lifted the knocker in the center and banged twice. Deep within, a hollow boom answered.

Looking around, Jermyn shivered. He didn't belong here—it was too quiet, too clean, too pretty. He missed the mud and the bustle of Riverbend.

"Aunt, let's go home," he said impulsively.

"Hush, boy."

A panel in the door opened, and a clear young voice called, "I'm sorry, we don't want any milk today."

Merovice frowned. "Then it's fortunate I'm not delivering any," she said crisply. "Tell your master he has guests."

"Oh," the same voice said. "Oh, I *am* sorry."

The panel closed, and the barrels of the great lock began to turn. The door opened to reveal a slim girl of about fifteen, with wheat-blond hair and amazingly deep brown eyes.

Jermyn gaped.

"I'm sorry," the girl said again, nervously. "We've been having trouble with the deliveryman, and I didn't know that Master Eschar had an appointment. At least—you do have an appointment, don't you?"

"We do not," Merovice said. "If you will tell your

master that Merovice Graves is here with her nephew to see him, then we will."

"Oh, dear." She hesitated, and pulled back slightly. "I'm afraid I'll have to ask you to wait out here. I think the Master's still at breakfast." She closed the door, leaving them standing outside it.

Merovice nodded her approval. "A well-trained girl—no sense letting strangers into the house until you're certain it's safe. Especially not the house of a wizard. And I don't mind a bit of a wait outside for form's sake either, though if her master really is at breakfast, it'll be the first time in years he's bothered to eat a decent meal in the morning." She went on: "More likely he'll have been up all night in his study—Jerry? What's the matter with you?"

"I never knew anyone could have blond hair and brown eyes like that," he said, dazed.

Merovice hid a smile. "It isn't uncommon in some parts of the world," she said noncommittally. "She's a pretty child, I must admit."

The door was opening again.

"The Master will see you now," the girl said, smiling at them warmly. "And I'm sorry about thinking you were the milkman, before. You won't tell him, will you? Master Eschar, I mean, not the milkman. He'll be disappointed in me, and there's really no harm done."

"Of course there isn't," Jermyn said, as warmly.

They were following her down a long, dim hallway, and he found himself trying to edge past Aunt Merry and closer to the girl. "We're in now, aren't we? And of course we won't—Aunt Merovice and I—won't tell on you."

"Thank you," she said, looking up at him in a way that made him want to do handstands. "I'm Meggan O'Loughlin—Master Eschar's ward."

"Are you, now?" Merovice smiled at her inscrutably. "Somehow I felt sure you weren't his student. A niece, perhaps? A cousin?"

The brilliant smile dimmed slightly. "No, nothing like that. My father commended me to Master Eschar's care when he died. The Master has been very kind to me."

"And I'm sure you must be a great help to him," Jermyn said stoutly.

Her smile came back full force, revealing a dimple in one cheek. "I try. Here we are, Mistress Graves. This is the Master's study. Shall I announce you?"

"No need, Meggie," said a deep voice from beyond the half-open door. "Merovice Graves learned her way around this house before you were born. Welcome, Merry. It's been too long."

Merovice preened. "Why, William, how kind of you to say so."

Jermyn choked. Aunt Merry called the Theoretician by his first name? But the person getting up from

56

behind the paper-strewn desk didn't seem so formidable, at that. Though he was a tall, saturnine man, long and lean, with a hawklike blade of a nose, there was untidy brown hair falling over one eye. His hands tapered like a musician's, and one of them held a bone pipe, half-filled. He was dressed in dark gray with a lighter gray over-tunic, very proper and ordinary-looking, but there was a hint of rumple about him, as if he had indeed been up all night reading one of the books that filled the shelves, tables, desks, and even the chairs of the room.

"Master Eschar," Meggan scolded, "I'd just gotten the books all neatly shelved on the back wall again, and now you've pulled half of them off!"

"I'm sorry, Meggan," he said repentantly. "I needed the Hortensius diaries, and I couldn't find them."

"You never *can* find what you want," she said, in fond exasperation. "Oh, well, never mind now—I'll straighten things later. Shall I light the fire?"

"Not just yet," he told her. "Though I would like to offer tea to our guests—or coffee, isn't it, Merovice?"

"You remembered," she said, pleased. "Yes, it is coffee, but not now, William. Business first, today."

"Very well. See to it that we aren't disturbed, Meggan. I'll ring when we want refreshments," Eschar said, smiling as the girl left. Jermyn watched her go with regret. "So this is Jermyn—don't look so startled, boy. I don't bite. You've grown since I saw you last."

"You wouldn't remember, Nephew," Merovice told him, the glint in her eye letting him know that he was expected to sit down and get hold of himself *at once*. "It was at your Naming, and you were about ten days old."

"And you cried incessantly and spit up all over my shirtfront," Eschar said amiably. "I think you've improved."

Merovice cast her eyes up to heaven. "Don't tease the boy, William. He's had a difficult time lately. In fact," and she hitched herself forward in her chair, "we both have, and it is too important for teasing."

"I felt sure that it was important," Eschar said pensively. "After all these years."

"Ah, well, you know how it is," Merovice said comfortably. "You get busy and all."

"I know how it is," he said, smiling again. "So tell me, Merry—what is the problem this time?"

"*This* time! I like that! And whose fault was it the last time we—" She started indignantly and then collected herself. "Well, never mind. It's like this—is that girl your apprentice? Or journeyman?"

"Meggan? No." He looked surprised. Score one for Aunt Merry. It heartened Jermyn to listen to someone else cope with her leaps of logic.

"Sure of that, now?"

"Very sure." He frowned, not pleased at the question. "She has no particular talent for magic, nor any need to earn her living—but that's none of your business, Merovice."

"It is, and all," she told him with a great air of candor. "For if you've already got an apprentice, you can't take on Jermyn."

"What!" The frown cleared, and he cast a quick, amused glance at Jermyn, who tried to look as if he were fascinated with the carpet.

"I want you to take Jermyn as your apprentice," she said. "I know you never take on more than one student at a time, but you're free now, and he needs a master."

"And who told you I was in the market for an apprentice?" he said, bemused. "I haven't taken one in years—I rarely even lecture, these days."

"I know," she said. "But no one else will take him."

Eschar looked at Jermyn again. "That's hardly credible. Merovice, perhaps we'd best—"

"Send the boy out of the room? Don't worry," she said coolly. "He knows it isn't his fault—it's all that slithering eel Fulke's doing. He's got every wizard in the city frightened to apprentice Jermyn—and I won't have it!"

"I knew you'd had trouble with Fulke again," Eschar said slowly. "It was the talk of the Court last midsummer. I didn't realize it was still going on."

"Well, it is, and all," she said. "Don't ask for details, because the matter is between Fulke and me, or should be. And don't say we should go to the Guild either, because we've no proof that would stand up before Council. Besides, I won't have it said that Jermyn needed to petition the Guild to find himself a master."

"Aunt Merry, I told you I don't mind," Jermyn said a little desperately. He wasn't certain what being a Theoretician's apprentice meant, but he felt certain, now that he saw the man, that he would be even worse at it than at everything else he had tried.

"You should mind," Eschar told him dryly. "It could destroy you, destroy your reputation as a wizard before it is ever established. What I don't understand, Merry, is why you don't teach the boy yourself. You're perfectly capable—"

"Not this time, I'm not. I'll own, I'd always planned on handling my nephew's apprenticeship myself, but we tried and it isn't working," she said starkly. "I'm doing Jermyn no good as his 'prenticemaster, and now, thanks to Fulke, I can't even find him a new one. Will you take him, William? For old time's sake?"

Jermyn focused on the carpet again. Merovice had warned him strictly before setting out that morning not to mention Fulke's curse. "For few people know, and I don't want the man to feel sorry for me, do you hear? If he hasn't heard, don't tell him," she had said, and he had to respect her wishes. It was hard enough for her to turn him over to a new master.

Eschar was looking troubled. "I really don't want an apprentice, Merovice. And I'm not likely to be much use to a practicing wizard."

"You can teach him the basics," she urged. "Teach him control—that's all I ask."

"Well, I don't know . . ."

"Please, William," she said, swallowing a little, and Jermyn had a feeling that the Theoretician knew perfectly well how much the plea cost her. "He has the talent. I can feel it in him. Let him get his independent license and there will be no stopping him."

He regarded her soberly. "You seem very sure of that."

"Well, of course I'm sure," she said, surprised. "Can't you see it in him yourself?"

"Of course I can't," he mimicked her. "I'm a theoretician, Merry. I leave judgments like that to you practicing wizards. Well, Jermyn, it seems that your aunt is determined to match us. What do you say to the matter?"

"He says yes," Merovice said before Jermyn could open his mouth.

"Peace, Merry. *You* aren't going to be my apprentice. Well, Jermyn?" The hooded eyes looked him over narrowly. "It won't be easy, you know. I assume you have a familiar?"

"I—yes—" Jermyn looked at his aunt nervously, then took the plunge. "Her name is Delia, and she—she's a skunk, sir, but I promise she won't be any trouble."

"A skunk familiar?" He looked a little surprised, but not upset. "Well, at least it's unusual."

"She—she wouldn't bother your familiar, sir," he repeated insistently, casting a dubious eye around the cluttered study. "And I'd see that she didn't come in here. With the books."

"You'd have to do more than that," he said coldly. "I do not have a familiar, nor do I permit such creatures in my home."

"What?" Jermyn opened his eyes wide. *A wizard without a familiar?*

Even Aunt Merry seemed taken aback. "What do you mean, you won't allow one in here? You've strengthened that since the old days, William."

"I have," Eschar agreed. "And with good reason. Most of our colleagues are overly dependent on the familiar-link to access their power. A particularly acute dependency during apprenticeship can lead to abuses which will limit a wizard his whole life long."

"Oh, tosh," Merovice said. "Just because you've grown too sour to appreciate a little furry company—"

"Merovice, if Jermyn is to be my apprentice, he must do things my way," Eschar said firmly. "And if he is to live here, he will have to wean himself from relying too heavily on his familiar's nearness. There will be a place for her in the garden—no closer."

"Live here?" Jermyn stared at the man. "I can't do that!"

"Most of my apprentices have lived with me," Eschar said calmly. "Why not? I will not take a student who is not committed to me."

"He's committed," Merovice said hastily. "Don't be a fool, Jerry—this is your best chance, unless you want to leave the city entirely."

"Aunt Merry, I won't!" he whispered behind one hand. "I can't leave you—the shop—"

"Don't you fret, boy," she said, though she was as pale as Eschar's pipe. "I managed the shop on my lonesome before you were born, and I can again."

"Not now, you can't," he insisted, too upset to worry about her pride. "There's Fulke's curse to worry about now."

"Curse?" Eschar said sharply. "What's this about a curse?"

"It's nothing," Merovice started, but Jermyn didn't give her the chance.

"Fulke cursed Aunt Merry," he said baldly. "Last summer."

Eschar's eyes narrowed again. "Merovice? Is this true?"

"It is," she said calmly, though the nervous twisting of her hands betrayed her. "What of it? Fulke and I have gone at it for years, William. I'd have mentioned it, but I thought you'd already know. You know all the secrets in this town."

"Not this one, evidently," he said grimly. "I've been busy. What's the extent of the curse?"

"Oh, not much. It's—"

"She can't finish a spell," Jermyn said for her. "When she tries, there's a backlash of psychic energy that overloads on her. If she tries too hard or too often, it starts to disrupt her—her life energy itself."

"*Then* what happens?" Eschar asked, though from the look in his eyes Jermyn thought he already had a fair idea.

"Well, I'm told my heart stops," Merovice said honestly, now that the truth was out. "Though I've no way of remembering, mind—"

"I remember," Jermyn said. "I was there, and it stopped."

"Yes, well, it started again." She took a deep breath. "The backlash disrupts my link to Pol, so I can't call on him to steady myself. Pol can feel me, but I sense him scarcely at all. I know you don't approve of the familiar-link, William, but it's a terrible thing to be cut off after having one."

"I don't doubt that it is, Merry," Eschar said gently. "And it isn't the familiar-link that I disapprove, but the misuse of it—which is not a factor in your situation. So Fulke managed a full blocking curse, then. That took a fair amount of strength even for a weather wizard with the full power of the storm behind him. Are all five basic nodes of power involved?"

"The full star," she nodded.

"Have you consulted anyone else?"

"One or two, in confidence."

Jermyn blinked, but his aunt only smiled at his surprise.

"Did you think me too proud to ask for help, Jerry? For all the good it did. It's a true Great Magic, William, and no one can solve it. I had hopes that I could break free with Jermyn to help me, since he's kin and we're close, but—"

Jermyn looked down, bitterly ashamed. "But I'm not good enough."

"Don't say that," she scolded.

"Why not?" he said, a little wildly. "It's true."

"If it were, you still shouldn't say it," Eschar told him. "And your aunt does not believe that it is true, and I trust her judgment. Merry, what did you do to get Fulke angry enough to take such a risk?"

She smiled wanly. "Oh, I set out to anger him, for one reason and another."

"For my sake," Jermyn said, in anguish. It was a relief to finally tell the truth to someone outside the problem. "She thought Fulke's attack on her might stimulate me to attach a familiar, and it did, but now—"

"Hush, Jerry. I succeeded too well, is the problem. He won't take the thing off without a public apology from me and the lad both—and that I will not do."

"I don't blame you," Eschar sighed. "You'd never live it down, in the Guild or beyond. It's a pretty puzzle, Merry—do you want me to try to research the curse for you? I might be able to find the answer."

"Might, might not," Merovice said with a fine show of unconcern. "I've made the mess; I can live with it, William. If you'd take Jermyn, I'd be grateful. Fulke won't dare threaten you."

"No. He won't," Eschar said. "So, boy, will you be my apprentice?"

"I won't leave Aunt Merry," he said firmly. "I may not be much of a wizard yet, but she needs me. Especially if—if Fulke gets even more angry. And anyway, Delia wouldn't be happy living in your garden."

"Is she happy in Riverbend?" Eschar asked casually, knocking the dottle out of his pipe into a green jade ashtray.

"Well—no," Jermyn said. He thought of Pol, and flinched. "But it's more like real country. She's happier there than she would be here."

"Very well." He stood up, suddenly seeming very tall. "It seems that you *do* have an acceptable reason, or reasons, for not boarding in this house. Therefore you will come to me in the mornings and return to the shop and your familiar by late afternoon each day. Skunks are nocturnal animals—she will not miss you. Much."

Jermyn's mouth fell open. "You mean—you'll take me? You think you can help?"

"I will teach you, boy," Eschar said irritably. "Whether or not you will learn, or if that learning will help—well, that we shall have to see."

5

THEORETICIAN'S APPRENTICE

THE FORMALITIES came first: the next morning, Jermyn and Merovice met Master Eschar at the house in Wisteria Street, to go with him to the Hall of Registry in order to transfer the apprenticeship. Delia had to come, too.

"Now, of course she has to be here," Merovice exclaimed as they waited in the front hall for Master Eschar to put on his cloak. "She's your familiar. She'll always be part of any contract you sign."

"But Master Eschar doesn't want her here." When Eschar himself opened the door, Jermyn had been conscious of a faint disappointment. He'd been hoping to see the girl Meggan again.

"In his house," Merovice said impatiently. "William knows the beast has to go with us today as well as you do, Jerry. What are you fussing at? She came last time we registered, didn't she?"

"Yes, but—" Delia had been only newly attached when they'd gone to the Registry with Merovice, Jermyn remembered uneasily. Exhausted, the little skunk had slept trustingly in his pocket the whole time. Now she was too big to sleep in his pocket, and wouldn't have consented to it in any case. He was carrying her tucked under his cloak when they arrived at Wisteria Street.

She poked a cold nose into his hand. *Go river?*

"No, we aren't," he said shortly, shivering. The day was overcast, and there was a hint of snow in the wind off the water.

Eschar paused with his hand on the door. "Did you say something?" he asked Jermyn.

"Uh, no, sir," he answered hurriedly, looking wildly at his aunt. "I was just telling Delia where we were going. She's curious."

The Theoretician frowned slightly. "Curiosity is a notably useful trait in a familiar. I commend you."

"Oh, the beast is useful enough," Merovice said so disparagingly that Jermyn's mouth tightened. "Come along, William, we'll be late."

"I didn't know we were expected," Eschar said, amused and distracted. Jermyn held his peace.

The Inns of Court were a muddle of red brick buildings just beyond the Royal Court proper—law courts were at one end, and the Chambers of Justice, with the Hall of Registry, were at the other. The Registry was where people went to record the major events of a life: birth, marriage, apprenticeship, licensing— or death.

Jermyn's arms tightened around Delia, and she squirmed. What was *wrong* with him? He hadn't felt this way when he'd come with Merovice. But then, he'd always expected to register as Merovice's apprentice someday. This was different.

His aunt was feeling it too, he could tell, but the bustle of the Registry Courtyard revived her. She took a deep breath, and looked around with satisfaction.

"This place never changes, does it?" she said happily. "Always busy."

"Too busy, sometimes," Eschar acknowledged, but he was smiling. "I have occasionally thought that we ought to rename the place Crossroads, and be done with it."

"Now, William," she scolded. "Just because you don't like crowds . . ."

Jermyn kept a firm grip on Delia. He had never particularly minded crowds, but he didn't like the thought of her panicking in this one. There were vendors in from the country, renewing licenses and plying their wares; there were courtiers strolling about, gossiping and making idle purchases; there was even a young couple in wedding finery, grouped happily with their attendants for a street artist to sketch.

"It's an aromatic experience, certainly," Eschar was saying.

Merovice didn't look at him. "Well, now, will you look at that nice fresh flounder. Just the thing for dinner—you'll join us, William? In honor of the occasion?"

She was off before he could answer. The Theoretician exchanged amused glances with Jermyn.

"*She* doesn't change either, does she?" he said. "Do you really think she means to go into the Registry carrying a rush basket full of fish?"

"She'll probably expect one of us to carry it," Jermyn said honestly. Delia was wriggling impatiently; he wished he could find a quiet place to set her down.

"Well, she's right about one thing," Eschar said. He was looking ahead, through the crowd. Jermyn craned his neck in that direction, but there were too many people in the way from where he was standing. "One never knows who will turn up in the Yard. Would you mind waiting here for your aunt? Tell her I'll only be a moment."

"No, of course I—" but Eschar was off before Jermyn had time to finish the sentence. He swallowed the rest of it and began looking for an open space near the wall, one with a good view of the center.

"Oh, pardon, sir, ma'am," he said, narrowly avoiding a middle-aged couple. The husband glared at him, but the wife smiled sweetly. "Oh, I'm so sorry—" That was to an older woman, ostentatiously crying into a black laced kerchief. "Beg pardon—so sorry, let me through, please."

He settled next to a pushcart filled with fruit, and prepared to wait. Delia poked her head out of his cloak curiously, and Jermyn firmly poked it back in.

No, he sent at her. *You stay where you are.*

She grunted slightly. *Looksee?*

After we get registered. Maybe. If you're good.

He was relieved when Merovice found him, though he groaned internally at the basket under her arm—and the string bag with loaves of bread dangling from her hand.

"Oh, *there* you are, Jerry," she said, as if he'd moved miles instead of only a few paces. "Look what lovely fish! Fresh and fat as baby piglets. Pol will be so pleased—and don't you look so sour, Nephew. You like my baked flounder almost as much as Pol does."

"Aunt Merovice, you can't go into the Registry Office smelling of fish!" he said desperately.

She looked affronted. "Well, I should hope not! I'll give it to one of the guardsmen to hold—they're quite used to minding parcels. Where's William?"

"He went that way," Jermyn said, jerking his chin for direction because he didn't want to let go of Delia.

The crowd opened slightly, and there was Master Eschar talking to a man of a little less than medium height and weight, wearing a cloak of dark blue satin that flared with a foreign cut.

"Who's that?" Merovice said, without great interest.

"I don't know," Jermyn said, wondering how she thought he would. "A friend of Master Eschar's, maybe."

"Strawberries!" his aunt said happily, discovering the fruit vendor. "We can have fresh strawberries for dessert."

"Aunt, we can't afford strawberries out of season," Jermyn was saying, when he suddenly became aware of an itchy feeling between his shoulder blades. The fruit seller, about to become an interested participant in their conversation, suddenly went silent and edged behind his cart.

Carefully casual, Jermyn turned his head to see who was behind him, and almost choked. It was Fulke. The Weather Master's little pointed beard was curled elaborately, and his ruddy complexion still clashed badly with the rose pink court dress that today he wore topped with an amazingly vivid purple cloak.

"Uh, Aunt Merry—"

"Well, I don't think a few strawberries will matter," she was saying crossly. "It isn't as though we were starving, you know. Yes, what is it?"

"I'm glad to hear you aren't starving, Merovice,"

Fulke said condescendingly, swirling his cloak behind him. "Though I don't suppose it would hurt any of us to lose a few pounds."

"Speak for yourself, you blowhard," Merovice snapped.

"I usually do," he said, flicking imaginary dust off a rose-silk sleeve. "Buying strawberries, are you? How very industrious of you to come all the way to the Registry to be sure of the highest quality. Now *I* am come to the Court on a matter of business, not to buy fruit."

"If you think I'm interested in your business, then either you were born stupid or all that thunder has gone to your head—neither of which would surprise me," she said, her nose in the air.

"You *should* be interested," he said, and his voice grated suddenly. "I've come to lay a complaint—against your apprentice!"

"Against me!" Jermyn stared openmouthed at the man, and then remembered. "Oh, no—Peter!"

So much had happened since the day before yesterday, that the encounter with Peter seemed part of the dim and distant past. Obviously the Weather Master didn't see it that way.

"Indeed," he said, scowling. "My journeyman will be unable to work for *weeks* because of your incompetence, snirp! A wizard—even a half-witted, lacktalented excuse for an apprentice—who can't control his familiar deserves to be—"

Merovice swelled. "Why, you—you overripe strawberry elf! This isn't about the skunk, and you know it!"

"Nonsense, of course it is," Fulke said. "Only you, Merry, would let your precious nephew attach such a ridiculous animal—"

Tired of being referred to as if he weren't present, Jermyn interrupted. "She wasn't so ridiculous last month," he said coldly. "When she chased you out of the shop. Was she—Weather Master?"

The way he used the title was in itself an insult. Fulke glared.

"You are impertinent, boy," he said loftily, but he glanced around as he said it. They were beginning to attract a considerable audience. "My consultations with your aunt are none of your concern."

Jermyn snorted. "Do you always consult herbalists after midnight? *And* wearing a cloak of invisibility?"

"Probably it was his idea of style," Merovice added. "Or perhaps he was trying to do us all a favor. It would certainly be easier on the eyes if that outfit he's wearing now were invisible."

That earned her a few snickers from onlookers, and Fulke almost gobbled his outrage.

"You plant-grubbing little—"

"Hello, Weather Master," said a dry, amused voice. "I see you are already acquainted with my new apprentice and his aunt?"

75

It was Master Eschar, and he'd brought the small-ish man in gray with him.

"Eschar!" Fulke deflated comically. He looked wildly at Jermyn. "Your—your new apprentice?"

Merovice was too angry to be distracted. "Yes, his new apprentice," she said. "And fortunate you are I don't drag you before Council for slander and calumny."

"Why, I've no idea what you mean, Merovice," Fulke said urbanely. He glanced sideways at Eschar, who merely smiled.

"Of course not," the Theoretician said blandly. "Merovice, Jermyn, might I present Blaine, Lord Dev-ereux, Marquis of Lumiansk? The Marquis is the cur-rent Lumianskan emissary to the Empire. Oh—and Weather Master Fulke, of course."

The dapper little man's nose twitched slightly—at the faint odor of fish, no doubt, Jermyn thought in some amusement—but he smiled and bowed to Aunt Merry like a courtier. "I am honored, Mistress, to make the acquaintance of you and your so charming nephew. And to renew my friendship with the Weather Master, who has been on my government's retainer for this past season."

"So I'd heard." Eschar looked Fulke up and down so thoroughly that the Weather Master almost wiggled. "One hears a great deal, even living retired as I do."

Lumiansk was one of the Continental treaty states, Jermyn knew, an independent principality owing fealty to the Empire for over two centuries. He'd never heard of any Guild wizard taking service with their sovereign, though.

The Marquis had turned back to Eschar.

"Does this mean that you are considering coming out of your retirement, friend Eschar?" he said, though there was no warmth in his voice. "If you are, then I have no doubt but that my prince would wish me to renew his offer of retainer."

"As before, I would not be interested," Eschar said shortly.

"But if you are taking apprentices again . . ."

"Yes, what about that, Eschar?" Fulke had found his voice. "If you are in the market for an apprentice, I could advise you on a likely lad or two—"

"Thank you, Weather Master, I have no need of your advice," Eschar said, his tone as cold as winter. Jermyn could have cheered; Merovice sniffed eloquently.

"You'd advise him after you're done laying your complaint against his current choice for apprentice, you mean?" she said to Fulke, sweetly.

Eschar frowned. "A complaint? Fulke, what is the meaning of this?"

"They've been harassing me," he said petulantly.

"My journeyman will be unavailable to me for weeks because of that brat and his—"

"Oh, poor Fulke!" Merovice said swiftly. "No journeyman with you for weeks. Why, you might even have to do some work yourself, for a change."

"Merry—," Eschar started, but Fulke had turned as purple as his cloak.

"How dare you!" he roared. "I'm a member of Council! You can't—"

"That, again," she said, lifting her chin dangerously. "I've told you before, Fulke, I do as I please and I always will."

At that moment, Delia decided that she'd had enough of being crammed into Jermyn's cloak like a bagged lunch. She squealed decisively, and poked her head out and downward, both forepaws resting firmly on Jermyn's arm.

Fulke goggled. "What's that creature doing here?"

"She's Jermyn's familiar, of course," Eschar said calmly. It was the last calm remark anyone made for some time.

Losing control completely, Fulke reached for Delia. Not liking the prospect of being touched by anyone but Jermyn, she hissed at him like a cat.

"Leave her alone," Jermyn said, trying to fend him off and hang onto his familiar at the same time. "She isn't doing you any harm."

Fulke grabbed Delia's head, and she immediately sank her teeth into his thumb. He howled, dancing backward, with her teeth still firmly fastened into his flesh. Unfortunately, he danced right into the Marquis, knocking the smaller man over. Looking startled, Eschar reached to help the Lumianskan just as Jermyn lost his grip on Delia. Simultaneously, she released her hold and fell to the floor with a little *thump*. Her tail quivered.

"Here, now, Jerry—," Merovice started, but she was laughing.

The Marquis didn't laugh. Face white with fury, he struggled to his feet.

"Fulke!" he said dangerously.

"Jermyn, control your animal," Master Eschar ordered. "Merovice, control *yourself*—"

Grimly determined, Delia grunted. Fulke, eyes popping angrily, gestured at her with one hand, and lightning crackled.

"No!" Jermyn cried, and incoherently flung up his hands.

There were bright colors in his mind, extending from vaguely imagined inscriptions to an equally imaginary mental horizon. Reaching out with his senses, he sought to extend the shimmering rainbow protectively over Delia, over Merovice and himself—over everyone but Fulke. But the colors were ragged and muddy, the arc had holes in it, and there was too much force. It touched Merovice and her basket, coming too close—

And then the nice fresh flounder exploded, as if the fish had died of eating firecrackers. Fragments of scales and meat cascaded over Fulke, Jermyn, Merovice, Delia, and assorted outraged and vocally appalled bystanders. The Marquis came in for his share—only Master Eschar missed the most of it, standing a little beyond and to the left of the explosion.

"Merovice!" Fulke choked, mottled with anger. "Not *again!*"

The smell of raw fish was thick enough to taste in the air; not even Delia could have done worse.

Two hours later, they were in the garden of Master Eschar's house on Wisteria Street, though Jermyn couldn't have given a coherent account of how they got there to save his life. He had a vague memory of clinging to a subdued Merovice with one hand and Delia with the other, while Master Eschar snapped quick orders at both of them. He couldn't even remember signing the Transfer of Apprenticeship. He must have done so at some point, though, since it was done.

He was the Theoretician's apprentice now.

In the garden, they drank tea and ate biscuits carried out to them by Mrs. Dundee, Eschar's housekeeper. Meggan was nowhere in sight, for which Jermyn was glad. He didn't feel up to facing her at the moment.

"At least now I see that your aunt wasn't being partial when she said you had talent," was the Theoretician's only direct comment to his new apprentice. "The power must be almost leaking out of your ears for you to lose control so spectacularly."

"I told you so," Merovice beamed smugly. She still smelled faintly of fish; so did Jermyn. So did Delia, who was busy investigating the fountain. Neither she nor Merovice seemed the least bit disturbed at having been called every bad name in the language and a few that weren't—or by the threat of being summarily hauled off to Justice to pay for their crimes. "What do you think his field will be? It isn't growing things, that I do know."

"Because it's your own? I supposed it was not, for that reason," Eschar said. "You would have been able to tell. As for what Jermyn's field actually *is*—at that level of power, it could be almost anything. I can tell you he's no theoretician, at least."

Jermyn flushed, then took the plunge. "Master Eschar, what am I going to do?"

"About what?"

"About—well, about losing control." He glanced down, but Delia wasn't paying attention. "If it isn't me letting go of some spell, it's—something else."

"A veritable round-robin of upset," Eschar said dryly. "I suggest you study, boy."

"Well, he knows that, William," Merovice said impatiently. "Do you have a course of study to recommend?"

"In fact, I do," the Theoretician said. "What do you feed your familiar?"

"What?" The abrupt shift of subject confused Jermyn. "Uh—oatmeal, mostly. Some milk and fruit."

"She isn't a fussy eater, I'll give her that," Merovice allowed.

"No wonder her fur is so dull. She ought to get meat at least once a day."

Jermyn was horrified. "You mean I haven't been feeding her right?"

Delia cocked her head at his distress; even Merovice looked perturbed.

"I never thought—William, have we been starving the beast?"

Eschar was soothing. "Not yet. She's young, and babies eat soft foods. But she is a carnivore, like all familiars. You should have known that, Merry, and so should your nephew have known it. Which means, Jermyn, that your first course of study with me will be to find out a few things about your familiar."

Merovice looked shocked. "You mean you're going to make him study *skunks?*"

"Why not?" Eschar smiled whimsically. "If the familiar-bond is to work effectively, then the wizard ought to know as much about the nature of his familiar as possible. Oh, don't look so disapproving, Merry. He'll learn a great deal about sorcery and magic in the process of learning about himself and his familiar. I promise you, he will learn a *very* great deal."

6

LESSONS

MASTER ESCHAR, Jermyn soon discovered, had a gift for understatement that bordered on the magical. From the moment a cheerful Meggan opened the door to Jermyn every morning—he always tried to time his arrival so she would be the one to let him in—until it closed behind him every afternoon, he worked. He had never worked so hard or learned so much in his life. He studied skunks, he studied the Theory of Similarities and Congruences, he learned the Laws of Science and Thaumaturgy by heart and by practical example, and then he learned the theory behind them. He even found himself studying the Royal Magic.

"But I'm not going to be a Priest!" he'd protested. "They're the ones who are responsible for the Royal Gift. Why do I need to know about it?"

"If you do not understand it, then you should examine it," Eschar had said uncompromisingly. "No magic—no person—exists in isolation. It is all a piece of the whole."

And then, of course, there was his daily tutoring session with Master Eschar, an hour first thing in the morning *every* morning—even on holidays. In fact, it was the question of the Royal Gift that first alerted him to just how different Master Eschar was as an apprentice-master.

"The Royal Gift is about growing things, isn't it?" Jermyn asked.

"Essentially, yes," Eschar said dryly.

"Then why is it so special?" Jermyn said curiously. "It's just like Aunt Merry's herb-lore. Why does it have to be inherited?"

The Theoretician raised one eyebrow. "An interesting point. You know, at one time it was believed that all magical gifts were inherited—that only the child of a weather wizard could be a weather wizard, for example."

"Yes, but we know better now," Jermyn said. "So why can't just anyone be born with the Royal Gift?"

"For one thing, the Ruler is rarely a wizard, of any sort," Eschar said. "The Royal Magic appears to function on a purely unconscious level, under the guidance of the High Priest. For another—why don't you find out?"

Which was how Jermyn found himself designing experiments to investigate the nature and effect of the Royal Gift. First he had to design an experiment to see what the Gift was—to evaluate its purpose, magical content, and effect on the land. Then Master Eschar put him to work testing various plants to see if he could detect the presence of *any* magic in them.

"Theoretically, the king's magic imbues the land itself and all the growing things thereon," he told Jermyn. "How?"

In short, Master Eschar's response to almost any question was to tell Jermyn to try to answer it himself. Where other masters simply told their apprentices what was what, Master Eschar said: "If you want to know, go and find out." It was extremely frustrating.

Master Eschar gave Jermyn a corner of the library to use as a workroom; as a theoretician, he didn't need much space for experiments, and the library was the center of his research. It was a big, comfortable room lined with bookshelves, with a door to the hall at one end and big, folding doors to the study at the other. There was a fieldstone fireplace on the long inner wall, flanked by shabby overstuffed leather chairs and a mismatched sofa. A long central table ran down the center of the room, and there were smaller tables in each corner; Jermyn used one as a desk. The outer wall had tall windows looking out onto the garden, with a glass-paneled door in the center and heavy green velvet drapes. Meggan had told him that it was a pleasant, airy room in the summer, but with the autumn storms upon them and the season turning even more gray and rainy than most, he was usually thankful for the fire.

He was working at his desk one morning about a month after he came to Master Eschar's, running yet another experiment on an oak sprig. He'd begged this one from a gardener at the Royal Garden. If any patch of ground in the city would show the influence of exposure to the Royal Gift, it surely ought to be the place where the ruling family had walked almost daily since the Court was built, Jermyn thought. He meant to compare this small spray of leaves to a sprig taken from an oak tree in the City Gardens—almost as venerable, but not as nobly patronized.

Wearing gloves, he laid the first twig on a clean sheet of white paper and shook silverdust all over it. Then he picked the thing up and set it in a brass dish, the dust coating its upper surface nicely. On the paper, the little branch lay outlined, every leaf clear in the dust. *So far, so good.*

He concentrated, and began to pull magic in from

the air around him. *Gently now, gently—not too much.* Yes, there was his link to Delia, slightly attenuated because his familiar was clear across town. The link glowed faintly, a thin golden cord leading outward from his mind. Carefully, he tested it, pulling power through it; the cord pulsed faintly with light —good. *Now in my mind I fill the empty spaces of the sprig outline with this same golden light,* he told himself, striving for calmness. *Only slowly, and even more carefully.* A transparent image of the sprig began to glow against the paper. Jermyn whispered the words of the spell, and then held his breath. In a moment, the light should begin to fade, leaving only the residue of magic contained in the sprig. If he could hold the flow of magic steady—

When the light shivered, he almost cried out. Desperately he fought to hang on, to *force* the spell back into focus, but it was no use. A soft *poof* sent the silverdust swirling into the air. The image of the sprig wavered, and then shriveled and faded away.

"Oh, Powers Above!" Jermyn said in disgust. "I thought I had it—"

"What happened, Jermyn?" Master Eschar's voice said behind him.

He turned wearily. "I lost the focus again, sir. As usual."

Eschar looked at the mess of silverdust on his desk. "Well, at least this time the paper didn't ignite. That's something."

"Not much." Moodily he went to get the fireplace brush and began to clean up. "And now it's all to do again."

"Have you learned anything from this test?"

"No—that is, I don't think so."

"Record your results, then, and go on." Eschar returned to the library shelves—he often came into the library for a volume, though he usually worked in the study.

"Excuse me, sir," said Mrs. Dundee, Eschar's house-keeper, from the study doorway. She was dressed for out-of-doors, Jermyn noticed, in a rain cape and boots— she must have been on her way to market when the bell rang. "Master Douglas is here to see you."

"Show him in here," Eschar said, turning from his books immediately. "I didn't expect to see you again so soon, Spellcaster. What brings you out on such a miserable day?"

Steen Douglas, the Master Spellcaster and head of the Council of Wizards, was a dry, withered, elderly stick of a man dressed in rusty brown. He'd been the Spellcaster since before Jermyn was born, and Jermyn thought that the man must be as old as the Empire itself. Now he settled himself into one of the library chairs with all the privilege of old age, and stretched out his mud-splashed boots to the fire.

"Ah, that's better," he sighed. "Old bones ache— nothing important, William. You can finish ticking off your apprentice first."

Eschar exchanged an amused look with Jermyn. "I was not ticking him off, Spellcaster. We were just discussing one of his experiments."

"Oh?" Douglas perked up. As a spellcaster—the branch of magic associated with "fixing" a spell onto its desired object—he tended to be more interested in theory than most practicing wizards. "What is he researching?"

Jermyn looked at Eschar for permission to speak, and received a nod.

"I'm looking into the Royal Magic, Spellcaster," he said decorously.

"So-ho!" Douglas chuckled, a sound like rustling leaves. "Infected the boy with your own preoccupations, Theoretician?"

"Jermyn chose his subject himself, Spellcaster," Eschar said calmly. "He's trying to evaluate the presence of the Royal Magic and of magic in general in the growing things of the city."

"Huh. What tests is he using?"

"He can also speak for himself," Eschar reminded Douglas mildly. "Apprentice?"

Jermyn took a deep breath. "I'm using the Amstellaer Similarity Test for the presence of magic, sir— at Master Eschar's suggestion."

Douglas's eyes widened. "Advanced work for a first-year apprentice."

"I am hardly a typical apprentice-master," Eschar responded.

"Yes, I'd wondered about that. It's been years since you've taken someone on," the spellcaster said, and leaned back with a sigh. "Ah, well, that's not what I'm here for. Did you have those numbers for me on the weather patterns yet? I'll need them for the next Council meeting."

"Yes, of course," Eschar said. "Jermyn, fetch the file on my desk, please."

It was a green box file, sealed and so light it couldn't have held anything but paper. "This, sir?"

"Yes, that's it." The Theoretician took it from him and handed it to Master Douglas.

"You didn't have to walk all this way just for this, Spellcaster. I could have sent it."

Douglas waved his hand. "I didn't walk far—picked up a hackney on the way, and told the driver to wait. An old man needs an occasional outing."

Eschar smiled. "Of course. It's a bit early for brandy—tea, then?"

"And some of Mrs. Dundee's fresh scones, I hope," Douglas said, smiling. "My healer'd have a fit. Woman's got me on a diet—for my heart, she says. *Pah!* There's nothing wrong with me but old age, and nothing she or anyone else can do about that."

Eschar nodded at Jermyn. "Tell Mrs. Dundee we'll want noon tea in the library."

"Yes, sir," Jermyn said, and went out the door to the hall.

Mrs. Dundee was waiting in the kitchen. She was

still dressed to go to market, but she had the tea tray ready. She was just pouring boiling water into the kettle. "I knew they'd want tea—it's early for brandy."

"Yes, ma'am." Jermyn's eyes went past her, searching the kitchen. "Do you want me to take it in for you?"

The housekeeper smiled knowingly, looking over her shoulder. There, standing at the washbasin up to her arms in soapsuds was—

Meggan. Her pale gold hair was tied back, leaving only tendrils to curl around her face, and she was flushed from the heat of the hot water she was enthusiastically sloshing over the breakfast dishes. For a moment, Jermyn lost track of Mrs. Dundee entirely.

"—take the tray in as I go," the housekeeper was saying, when he recovered. "You can help Meggan with the washing up while I go to market, there's a good lad."

"Yes, ma'am," Jermyn said, abashed. Meggan smiled at him mischievously, and his heart turned over.

Helping Meggan with the housework was often the high point of his days. She was bright, funny, gentle, so beautiful he almost couldn't stop looking at her, and totally unlike the girls he had known in Riverbend. Somehow Meggan inspired him with a desire to protect her—she seemed so vulnerable. And she didn't seem to mind his company, either. In fact, once or twice he'd caught her looking at him with a sort of wistful expression in her dark eyes, as if maybe she even liked him a little. At least she claimed to find him helpful, which he believed was only because—astonishingly—she was also as clumsy as Delia.

He took a dish towel and joined her at the basin. Striving to be casual, he said: "Hello, Meg. Haven't seen you in a while."

"Since yesterday," she said, and her smile deepened.

"That's a while," he said stoutly.

Meggan was rarely at a loss for words. Quickly changing the subject, she asked brightly: "Who's in the study with Master Eschar?"

"The Spellcaster—Steen Douglas. He was here the other day."

"Oh, him." She sniffed. "I remember. He spilled the brandy, and I had to go in and clean it up before it stained the rug. How's Delia?"

"She's fine," Jermyn said.

"Did the shoulder pad work? Oh!" There was a crash. Jermyn looked up sharply. "Oh, well, it wasn't one of the *good* plates."

"Cut yourself?"

"Not this time," she said impatiently. "What about the shoulder pad?"

"I haven't tried it yet." He was tempted to offer

to trade jobs with her, but knew from experience that wasn't a good idea; Meggan occasionally broke dishes while washing up, but when she tried to wipe slippery plates and put them on shelves, the result was china carnage. Things simply flew out of her hands, sometimes clear across the room. Mrs. Dundee had taken to hiding the glassware.

"If it does work, maybe we could go on a picnic together."

"No," she said, and her voice was suddenly flat.

"The weather's still warm enough," he persisted, delighted at the prospect. "We could wait for a nice day and go out along the river. Dee loves the river, and we could ask Aunt Merry and Master Eschar—"

"I said no!"

There was a brief silence; Meggan busied herself with her soapsuds, while Jermyn tried not to feel hurt.

"I'm sorry," he said at last, humbly. "I—I didn't mean to presume."

"You didn't. Not really." She bit her lip, and pushed a strand of gold hair back over one ear. "Couldn't you bring Delia here?"

"I suppose so," he said dubiously, and then brightened. "Master Eschar did say once that she could stay in the garden. I could bring her with me one morning, and she could stay outside."

Meggan clapped soapy hands. "There, you see? We could picnic by the fountain, just the two of us.

Wouldn't that be nicer than some old crowded riverbank?"

"What about tomorrow? Oh—there's the bell." From the front of the house came a silvery ring, amplified by a local echo spell. "You or me?"

Meggan listened for a moment. "You, I think— yes, there's the second one. He must want someone to fetch the tea things. You'd better go. I can finish myself."

"Don't you dare!" Jermyn said, relieved that things were back to normal between them. "Set them on the drainboard, and I'll take care of them later. Or Mrs. Dundee will when she gets back from market."

She dimpled at him. "Silly. I can certainly put away a few pieces of china."

"That's the problem," he reminded her. "The number of *pieces* they'll be in if you put them away. Why don't you go make the beds?"

"Oh, all right." She giggled. "I suppose I can't break a feather pillow. Oh, go away, Jermyn, do— your master's calling."

"I'm on my way."

He tossed his towel over a chair and headed for the library. The shoulder pad Meggan had reminded him about was her idea. One day when he'd been complaining about having to carry Delia everywhere they went together, she'd suggested stitching a soft leather pad which could be tied to the outside of his tunics. Delia's claws weren't curved enough to catch on ordinary clothing without creating snags, but this might give her something to hang on to so that she could ride on his shoulder when he went about his errands. She'd like that, and it would give her a chance to become more accustomed to crowds. It had been kind of Meg to think of it.

Why didn't she want to go on a picnic? he wondered, still puzzled. *Did she think it wouldn't be proper? But we would have asked Master Eschar for permission. She couldn't think I'd want her to sneak out against her guardian's will. Could she?*

No, of course not. She wouldn't be so silly. She just didn't want to go, was all—Meggan seldom left the house. Well, so he'd just have to bring Delia to her.

The library was empty, and the double doors between it and the study were closed; the empty tea tray sat forlornly in front of the fireplace. Jermyn frowned at it. Why had Master Eschar taken his guest into the study and closed the doors? Thoughtfully Jermyn went back down the hall to the study's separate door. He wasn't sure what he expected, but he knew enough to be careful.

Despite his good intentions, Jermyn gawked like a loon: seated in the red leather chair in front of Master Eschar's desk was the elegant, polished Marquis of Lumiansk. Of Master Douglas, there was no sign.

"Sherry, Jermyn," Master Eschar ordered. "And bring the modern translation of Arnulf's *Syntagmatica*—the one bound in blue leather."

"Yes, sir," Jermyn said stiffly. He poured the sherry carefully, using the good crystal. When he set the tray down at Eschar's elbow, his master nodded approvingly.

"I told you before, Marquis, I am not interested in accepting your prince's retainer," Eschar was saying. "I am quite happy as I am."

"No doubt, no doubt." The man waved the brandy glass under his nose and sniffed delicately. "Ah! A fine wine, this."

"Thank you." Eschar inclined his head slightly. "A gift from a client."

"If you will take gifts from others, why do you persist in refusing my prince's most generous offer?"

"I have occasionally been of service to others," Eschar corrected smoothly. "Always in specific instances and for a specific purpose. Your prince wishes to place me on permanent retainer, to oversee his interests at Court—a place where I rarely venture, these days."

"But you will be established there again," the Marquis argued. "You were a confidant of our young Ruler's father, and when the Princess has attained her majority—"

"Many things will change, then," Eschar said,

standing up. Jermyn silently handed him the book he had requested. "Thank you, Jermyn—give it to the Marquis, if you please. He is borrowing it."

Reluctantly the Lumianskan finished his sherry and accepted the book. "I thank you for your kindness in this, at least, Master Theoretician. I had not believed that Arnulf was available in modern translation."

"The city bookshops are well supplied with his works, I believe," Eschar said coldly. "Though of course I am delighted to be able to lend you the words of your distinguished countryman."

"Of course, of course." The Marquis did not look obliged. He turned to Jermyn. "I wonder if I might have something to wrap the volume in? The rain is rather harsh, and I would not like to damage the binding."

"Jermyn, fetch a towel," Eschar said, unsmiling.

Outside the study, Jermyn abandoned his dignity and skittered down the hallway.

"Quick," he gasped to Meggan, who was fortunately still in the kitchen. "A towel—no, not that one! A clean towel."

"What for?" she said, at a loss. "Did that old wizard spill tea this time?"

"Who? Oh, Master Douglas—no, he's gone already. The Marquis of Lumiansk needs something to wrap a book in. You remember, I told you about him—from the Registry. He's in the study now. Master Eschar must have answered the door himself."

"You'd better hurry," Meggan said anxiously. "If the master's willing to lend the man a *book* to get rid of him, he must really want him gone."

"It's only a translation," Jermyn protested. "I'm going, I'm going—"

Passing the front door again, he peeked outside. Yes, there was a carriage waiting, with very damp outriders standing dripping in gray livery. So the Marquis had had no need to ask for something to wrap the book in; it would be dry in the carriage. He must have wanted a few more moments alone with Master Eschar.

Whatever he'd planned, it hadn't worked. When Jermyn entered the room, as carefully dignified as if he hadn't just raced down the hallway, Eschar was standing up against the bookcase. His face bore the absolutely expressionless look that Jermyn had come to recognize as anger. The Marquis was still seated in his chair, but he didn't really look comfortable.

He stood up as Jermyn entered. "A prompt apprentice is beyond rubies. I compliment you, Master Theoretician. This is young Wizard Graves, is it not? We met at that—rather aromatic occasion at the Registry."

Jermyn darted a quick look at his mentor. "Yes, sir. Jermyn Graves."

"And you, apprentice, are fortunate to have so forgiving a master." At the sting in the words, Jermyn flushed slightly. "I kiss your hands and feet."

Jermyn gulped. "Uh, thank you, sir."

"Show the Marquis out, Jermyn," Eschar said woodenly.

"Yes, sir."

One doesn't hustle a noble guest to the door, but Jermyn came as close to it as he dared. When the door closed behind the Lumianskan, he stayed glued to the peephole for a moment, waiting for the carriage to roll away. Not until the street out front was empty again did he return to the study.

Master Eschar was sitting at his desk with a book open in front of him, but he was staring at the pages unseeingly. Jermyn cleared his throat.

"Sir?"

"What? Oh, Jermyn." He closed the book. "Devereux safely seen off the premises?"

"Who?"

"Sorry—the Marquis, I should say. Blaine, Lord Devereux is his family name." Eschar looked at him curiously. "Didn't you realize?"

"I'd forgotten you said his name was Devereux," Jermyn admitted. "You always call him the Marquis, never Lord Devereux—or should it be Lord Blaine?"

"You were right the first time," the Theoretician said. "In fact, he uses his patrilineal designation far more consistently than his title of Marquis, though I am not entirely certain why he does so. However, since he prefers to be called 'Lord Devereux,' I am very careful not to do so to his face. It irritates him, and an irritated man is often unwary. Now, for pity's sake, apprentice, do not go repeating *that* little tidbit to all and sundry!"

"No, sir," Jermyn said, hastily wiping the grin off his face. "Uh, I think I should tell you—he had a carriage waiting."

"I never doubted it," his master said. "At least, not once I noticed how clean of mud his boots were."

"Yes, sir," Jermyn said, chastened. "Um, what happened to Master Douglas?"

"He left before Devereux arrived." Eschar sighed. "My old friend grows more and more frail, I'm afraid."

"Yes, sir," Jermyn said, respectfully. "Will you be needing me anymore today?"

"No, you can be off. Oh, and tell Meggan I want her, will you? She's gone and alphabetized my reference materials again, and I can't find anything."

"I'll tell her, sir, but I think she's making the beds."

There was a sudden bang from the upstairs, as if some small piece of furniture had hit the floor, and then an almighty *crash*. Eschar looked at the ceiling and sighed a long-suffering sigh.

"So I hear. Perhaps we'd better not disturb her just now. I'll see you tomorrow, boy. Give your aunt my best."

Jermyn was grinning again as he let himself out the front door. For all his sighs, Master Eschar was very fond of his ward. He might tease her, but Jermyn knew he really appreciated how much she wanted to help.

Pulling in his cloak against the cold, Jermyn trudged home. The steady light drizzle of early morning had given way to torrents: he'd be soaked in moments. Head down, he plodded forward doggedly. It was tempting to run, but the streets were mud a handspan deep, and slippery.

He was so intent on watching his footing that he didn't see the carriage until he'd almost bumped his nose on it. Gasping, he put out his hands to steady himself. What was this thing doing standing in the middle of the street? Then he saw the crest on the opening door.

"Why, it's young Wizard Graves," said Blaine, Lord Devereux, Marquis of Lumiansk. "And walking in the rain, too. Do let me offer you a ride."

7

A LARMS

JERMYN TOOK an involuntary step backward, but a liveried outrider had moved in behind him. Another held the door invitingly.

"No thank you," he started to say, but the Marquis cut him off.

"I insist." His smile was as cold as the rain.

There was no place to go but in. Gulping, Jermyn swung himself through the door, which closed smartly behind him. He settled himself on the front seat, riding backward and facing the Lumianskan.

"Thank you," he said politely. The warmth of the

carriage was very welcome—his quick eyes noted a brazier burning beneath the seat. "It *is* cold outside."

"Indeed," Devereux said meaninglessly. "Are you on an errand for Master Eschar?"

"Uh, no. I'm through for the day." Jermyn was conscious of a complete reluctance to tell this man just where he was going. "If you'd drop me by the south wharf, that would be fine."

The Marquis nodded, and banged on the carriage roof. The driver opened the trap, listened, and shut it when he'd heard his instructions. Jermyn noticed that the man carefully kept the hole in the roof shielded so that the rain didn't fall in on his employer—well-trained servants, these Lumianskans.

"It is fortuitous that we came up with you," Lord Devereux was saying. "I have been wishing for an opportunity to speak with you privately."

Now why doesn't that surprise me? Jermyn thought.

Aloud he said, as ingenuously as he could: "With me, lord? I'm honored. Whatever for?"

"I had hoped to place a small business proposition before you," the Marquis said.

"Really?" He did his best to look as excited as any apprentice offered the rare chance to earn an outside fee. "I'd be delighted—anything I can do—that is, provided my master approves."

"Oh, I'm sure we needn't mention this to your

master," the man said persuasively. "It's only a small matter, after all."

Jermyn's eyes narrowed slightly. Something about this didn't smell right. Surely this was early in the conversation for him to be offered a bribe? Unless the man thought he was a complete idiot. But the Marquis had Fulke on retainer, didn't he? And Fulke's opinion placed Jermyn somewhere below a catatonic angleworm when it came to intelligence. *Yes, that might explain a few things*, Jermyn thought.

"I couldn't, lord," he said firmly. "It's against the rules."

There, let the man deal with the stupidity of blind obedience.

The Marquis looked taken aback, but only for a second. Then the smile returned.

"You Westerners! Always so impatient," he said, shaking his head in patently false admiration. "I have told my good friend the Weather Master that it is impatience which has built this empire of yours—but surely, you could at least listen? It would hurt nothing to listen."

"Well . . ." Curious, Jermyn allowed himself to be persuaded. It wasn't as though he had much choice, anyway. "I guess not. All right, I'm listening. Lord."

The Marquis didn't seem to mind the unenthusiastic response. He talked for a good five minutes as the carriage jounced over some of the city's more rutted streets. They could have gone fully five times around the marketplace by now, all the way to the south wharf and back again, but Jermyn didn't pay much attention. At first, Devereux's proposition was about what he'd expected: cash in exchange for information about Master Eschar's doings—"purely on an informal basis, so that my prince might gauge his next offer more accurately, and more pleasingly." Then things got blurry. There was something about the rain—and an errand—and Fulke? He wasn't sure exactly when the world got fuzzy at the edges, or when he realized that something was seriously wrong. Perhaps it was when the carriage began to seem too warm, and the soft velvet cushions became suffocatingly deep. There was the hint of incense in the air, too, which made it hard to breathe. The Marquis held up a silver coin, and Jermyn squinted to look at it.

"You see," said the quiet voice at the edges of the light, "it really is a very small matter . . ."

The coin seemed to glow inside the dimness of the carriage. Half hypnotized, Jermyn reached for it—and in the back of his mind he heard a warning, familiar grunt and the pungent memory of a foul odor stronger, fresher, and more intense than all the perfumes ever made. He choked, and clenched his outstretched fist in the Marquis's face.

"What—what am I—what are you—" He turned furious eyes on the Marquis. With a quick slap he pushed the inviting hand aside, and the coin fell ring-ingly against the carriage door. "How dare you! It's against the law to use Persuasion against a citizen of the Empire."

The Marquis drew back.

"You are overwrought, boy," the Lumianskan said crisply, his pale eyes startled and wary. "I mean only kindness."

"I haven't lived with a Guild Mistress my whole life without learning what a spell looks like," Jermyn said, as angry as he'd ever been. "And Persuasions are illegal, except under special circumstances."

"I assure you, I am no wizard. Driver!" He rapped the roof sharply. "What is taking so long? Why have we not arrived?"

The carriage picked up speed.

"Tell him not to bother," Jermyn said grimly. "I'm getting out of here. You, driver! Stop—stop now!"

He reached for the handle, and the door fell open just as the carriage slewed around a corner. The Mar-quis almost snarled at him as the fresh air and rain blew inside, and Jermyn could have laughed in exhil-aration. He lunged forward and was outside—face-down in the mud, but outside—before the carriage had finished turning the corner. It did not slow down. One of the outriders reached down and slammed the door shut in a single motion, and then the carriage was gone.

Slowly, Jermyn stood up, brushing off the mud as best he could. He was in the marketplace, not far from the vegetable stalls. A pushcart vendor was coming up to him with an indignant expression on his face.

"Well, I never!" he said. "Bloody toffs think they own the street. Splashed water all over me, too. Here, are you all right? I saw what he did, pushing you out of the carriage like that."

"He didn't push me," Jermyn said, fair-mindedly. "I jumped."

"Well, must have had good reason, didn't you? And he didn't slow up, did he? Bloody toff." The vendor was determined to hold on to his grievance. "I'd get the law on him, I would. Got no right—"

"No," Jermyn said. "But I'm all right, and it *was* my own fault, in a way. Look, I had a pair of gloves in my belt—did you see where they went?"

"Saw the whole thing, I did," the man said. "You're the herbalist's boy, ain't you? Know her— good woman, that. Gave my missus a right good syrup for the cough when our little girl was sick. You want I should go fetch her?"

"My aunt? No," Jermyn said quickly. "Just help me look for my gloves, will you? I'd be grateful."

" 'Course I will," the man said, though he didn't move. "No trouble. I've not much else *to* do but look, in all this rain. Bloody incompetent weather wizards, make us nothing but rain for days on end. It keeps folks in so they don't buy but from door-to-door, and what's the rest of us to do, I ask? What's to do?"

"I don't know," Jermyn said, locating his left glove in a puddle and shaking the water out of it. *Now where did the right one go? Oh, behind me.* "You could take it before the Guild, I suppose."

The vendor almost sneered. "And who up there'd pay any attention to the likes of us? The working wizards, they know what we're up against trying to earn a living, but the Council? *Pah!* Bloody incompetent stiff-necked toffs—here, boy, this yours? Saw it fall when you did. Must be yours."

He held out one callused hand. In it, gleaming even through the mud, was the Lumianskan's silver coin.

"Saw the flash of silver," the vendor said righteously. "'Tisn't mine. Must be yours. 'Sides, it's some foreign bit, ain't it? No use to the likes of me. You wizards now, you likes a bit of foreign coin to work your magics with. Or so I'm told."

"Yes, we do," Jermyn said absently, taking the coin. It must have fallen out of the carriage with him. "Thank you. I'd offer you something in exchange, but I'm afraid I don't have much."

"Ah, no mind, lad." The vendor grinned, showing the holes in his smile. "Only an apprentice yet, ain't you? Well, we working folk, we got to stick together. You remember me when you earn your master's staff, that's all I ask. Ta, now. Mind you, stay out of strange carriages."

The coin shimmered in Jermyn's hand. On one side was the profile of a man; on the other, deeply incised and intertwined letters: an *M* and an *L*, ornately flourished. He'd never seen a coin quite like it before. For one thing, it was larger than most, especially in silver—at least, he thought it was silver. Frowning, he shoved the thing into his pocket. Maybe Aunt Merry would know exactly what it was.

8

DIVERSIONS

AUNT MERRY did, but first he had to calm her down. She was that furious.

"How dare he!" she said, white with anger. "Jumped-up little Continental, calls himself a lord—how dare he try to set a Persuasion on *my* nephew."

"Now, Aunt Merry," Jermyn said placatingly. "It didn't work, after all. What kind of coin is it, anyway? I don't recognize it."

She turned the silvery disk in her hands, and tested it against her teeth. "Huh—filthy Lumianskan white gold."

"What's that?" Jermyn said, taking it back from her. "I thought gold was yellow."

"It is," she said, her mouth narrow. "White gold's a special sort—you don't find it much on this side of the water, but they refine a lot of it in Lumiansk. Nasty-looking stuff, I've always thought. And that petty princeling's picture on it—"

Curious, he looked at the picture on the coin. "You mean it is Lumianskan currency, and that's the prince? But this is a young man, and I always thought the prince of Lumiansk was—um—quite old."

"One foot in the grave and doddering for decades," she told him. "Their coins aren't spelled against counterfeiters like ours, so that the image ages with the ruler. And that's coin of the realm in Lumiansk, if not many places else. Why they don't use good Western gold like everyone else—"

"Well, why don't they?" he asked, relieved that he seemed to have distracted her.

"Oh, because of the treaty. They've their own laws in Lumiansk, and their own church too. Their church says magic's illegal, so they don't have an honest wizard to their names—only boughten magics and hedgewitches and black artists the like of which the Guild won't permit. They've a lot of foolish Old Country superstitions, too, more than the worst of the back country on this side—the Continent is rife with such things. Our ancestors never did a better day's work than when they came to this new land, Jerry, and don't you forget it!"

"I won't," he said, and then added incautiously: "Though the Marquis seems to be doing all right for himself."

" 'Marquis,' is it!" she raged all over again. "A bunch of schemers, the lot of them, and he the chief snake. Well, I tell you, we'll be taking this to the Guild this very day. How dare he—"

"Aunt Merry!"

"—my own nephew, my only living flesh and blood, near bespelled on his innocent way back to his own home—"

"Aunt Merovice!" he said loudly. "Do you really think we ought to go to the Guild with this right away?"

At least it made her stop and look at him. "Why, of course, Jerry. You've the coin and the vendor's story—there'll be a trace of magic on the thing yet, enough to lay a complaint."

"Yes, well, shouldn't I see what Master Eschar has to say about it first?"

She froze. "I—forgot. Of course," she said in a hurt voice. "He's your 'prentice-master, not me. You'd best take his advice."

"I didn't mean—" He tried to mend matters, and only made them worse. "I just think he ought to know about the Marquis and all. It's his business."

"Yes, it is," she said, and busied herself with the herbs she was bundling on the counter. "Of course you must tell him. You shouldn't even have mentioned it to your poor old aunt."

There was just enough reproach left in her voice to make him squirm. He hadn't meant to hurt her feelings, but he obviously had. For all it had been her idea, she still had mixed feelings about sending him to Master Eschar. As he had himself, at first. "Aunt Merry, I did ask your advice just now. Didn't I?"

She didn't look up. "Of course you did, Jerry, and very kind of you it was, too. Mind, I always thought you'd be my student one day, at least for your apprenticeship, but it didn't work out and that's that. It's for the best for both of us, no doubt."

"Aunt Merry, I—" Sighing, he gave up. "Well, I'll take the coin to Master Eschar this evening, then."

"In this rain?" she said, swinging to look at him.

"Yes, in this rain," he told her firmly. "You're right—no sense putting things off."

"You could use the crystal—but then, there's no one in that house with enough practical magic to respond, now is there? Well, at least you'll eat something before you go, and have something hot to drink," she fussed. "And tend your animal. The poor beast is pining for you."

In fact, Delia was more worried than pining. She'd been waiting for him inside the shop door, where she was not usually allowed in case a customer came in and took fright at the sight of her. As soon as he swung the door wide enough, she had nuzzled his boots, completely ignoring the wet mud dripping off them. He'd been forced to brush her dry before doing much else, and even now she showed a marked disinclination to move away from him. She sat beside him on the other shop stool, her beady black eyes fixed firmly on his face.

"What's wrong with you?" he said to her irritably. "It's nothing serious—I just have to go out again for a little while."

Bad Je'm'n, her mind-voice said firmly. *Bad Je'm'n stay.*

Had she sensed something of what had almost happened in the carriage? He suddenly remembered the way the spell had failed, and wondered. Merovice wondered too, when he told her.

"It could be," she said stiffly; he was clearly not yet forgiven. "The familiar-bond works two ways. If she sensed you were going under, she might have reacted. What did the foreigner do, exactly?"

"You mean, what passes did he make?" Jermyn asked, and grabbed an apple from the bowl on the counter to munch on. "None that I saw—he just talked. It didn't seem to be a very serious Persuasion, Aunt—just something to make me willing to listen."

"Listen to what?"

He shook his head, frustrated. "The usual, I think. He wanted me to spy on Master Eschar, on his comings and goings, I remember that. There was something else, too, something I almost remember—like a picture in my mind."

"A picture?" Merovice frowned, but with professional puzzlement this time. "Of what?"

"Something sort of dark and long, and blocky-looking." He shook his head. "I keep thinking that I ought to recognize it, but that's all—the spell kept putting me to sleep."

"Odd sort of Persuasion, that."

"Uh-huh," he said indistinctly around a mouthful of apple. "It didn't seem to be working too well. I think the Marquis was as surprised as I at what happened."

She snorted. "And *I'm* not surprised at that. Him and his hired magics. He probably knows less about them than—than that skunk."

"Um." Thoughtfully he finished the apple and tossed the core to Delia, who wasn't so concerned about him to fail to catch it neatly in her teeth. "I suppose if you have money to hire people, you don't need to be much of an expert yourself. That must be why the Marquis has wizards on retainer—like Fulke."

"Without doubt," Merovice said, more cheerfully. "Always more money than they know what to do with, the Lumianskans—more gold than sense, as they say. And if Fulke doesn't stop concentrating on the gold and tend to his duties, he won't be Weather Master much longer."

"I was wondering about that," Jermyn said, with satisfaction. "Aunt Merry, just how strong is Steen Douglas? He stopped by the house for a visit this morning, and Master Eschar said he seemed frail."

She pursed her lips, looking at him with the hurt temporarily forgotten. "How strong is the Spellcaster? Well, now, that's hard to say. He's an old man. No worse than he has been, I should imagine, which might mean he's not so far from retiring. You were thinking of who is to head the Council when he's gone?"

He nodded. "And wondering if a Weather Master had ever been elected to the headship. I know it's usually the ranking Spellcaster, but Master Douglas's journeyman is still sitting his exams, isn't he? And there isn't anyone else in the city."

"That's so," she admitted. "Though I doubt that the vote would go to Fulke. He hasn't the politics for it. They'll probably bring in one of Douglas's former students who's made master. He has them all around the Empire, Powers know. Still and all, that might be in Fulke's mind. The old blowhard."

"And it might be why he has such a need of gold," Jermyn said suggestively. "White gold or otherwise."

Her eyes narrowed. "Now, there is a thought,

boy. A nasty one, but definitely a thought. Perhaps you'd best mention it to your master, when you go to ask his advice."

"Yes, Aunt," he said, rebuked again. He slipped off the stool and carefully set Delia down on the floor. "I'd better move, if I'm going to get back before dark. Did you get the straps sewn onto my tunic?"

"For the pad? I did that," she said. "Why? You aren't going to take the creature with you, are you?"

"Not today. I'd have to leave her sitting outside in the garden while I talked to Master Eschar, and it's raining too hard for that. If I try out the pad at home, though, I could bring her with me tomorrow. Meggan wants to meet her."

Aunt Merry smiled at him roguishly. "And what a pretty girl wants from you, she gets, is that it?"

"Aunt Merry!" he protested, uneasily aware of the color rising in his cheeks. "It isn't like that. Meggan's just—just a friend."

"A pretty friend," she teased, then frowned at him. "Why so serious, Jerry? You haven't been bothering the child, have you?"

"Of course not!" As if he would. "Only—well, she's strange sometimes."

"Strange how?"

"The way she doesn't like to leave the house. She doesn't even go into the garden very often," he said. "Today I asked her if she'd like to go on a picnic—

all of us, not just her and me—and you'd have thought
I asked her to go to the moon."

"Well, that's not so strange, lad," his aunt said
tolerantly. "She's young, and the city's a fearsome
place to those who aren't accustomed to it."

"Why wouldn't she be accustomed to the city?"
he asked. "She lives here."

"*Now*, yes, but she hasn't been here for long.
You just have to look at that hair to know—" She
paused, and almost visibly changed her mind. "If your
master hasn't told you, then perhaps he does not think
it any of your business."

"But—"

"Now, Jerry, you know better than that. So long
as you're going upstairs anyway, would you mind just
taking the biscuits out of the oven for me? They should
be browned by now."

"Yes, Aunt," he said, and headed into the back.
He knew there was no more to be learned from Aunt
Merovice this afternoon. Maybe later, when she'd
fully forgiven him, she'd be more forthcoming.
"Come on, Deedee—don't sulk. We'll try out your
new carry-pad upstairs, and if it works I'll take you
for a walk down by the river later."

Rain, the skunk said lugubriously. She tucked her
head between her feet and put her forepaws over her
nose.

"Yes, rain, but Master Eschar says you have to

exercise several times a week now that winter is coming on, or else you'll get sluggish and start to hibernate. Don't worry, I'll wear the heavy cloak."

"Still studying skunks?" Merovice said after him as he went through the door, her voice sour.

"Yes, well, it's interesting," Jermyn said defensively.

Pol, seated on the counter next to Merovice, opened and closed his amber eyes in a superior fashion, as if to say: cats don't hibernate, nor do they have to go out in the rain if they don't want to. Jermyn was amused to notice that Delia was deliberately ignoring the cat, scuttling after her master as if he and she were completely alone.

What was it that Aunt Merry had been about to say about Meggan? Jermyn wondered. *Well, maybe it really isn't any of my business.*

Upstairs, Jermyn slipped the tunic over his head and eyed the straps doubtfully. *Will they be strong enough? Only one way to find out.* As Delia watched interestedly from the floor, he fastened Meggan's pad over the back and shoulder of the tunic, tying it into place. *There, that isn't too uncomfortable, and the brown leather looks all right too.*

Turning this way and that in front of the mirror, he examined the lay and fit of the thing, until Delia poked his shin imperatively.

"Oh, you want to get up, do you? Well, here we go."

He lifted her into place against his shoulder, with her tail hanging down over his back. For a moment she scrabbled for purchase, then settled with her rear claws firmly set into the leather just above his shoulder blade and her forequarters resting on his shoulder. She hummed slightly with pleasure, her tail lifting jauntily so that he could see it in the mirror like a banner. He tried a few steps; she swayed, but held firm.

"How about that?" he said, delighted. "It works!"

Delia chortled at him. She rode downstairs on his shoulder, bouncing happily with every step. He had to walk carefully at first, adjusting his weight to account for the new burden, but it wasn't really difficult. No harder than wearing a knapsack, anyway.

"Aunt Merry?" he called as he walked through the open door to the outer shop. "Aunt Merry, come and look. It works!"

Too late he realized there was a customer in the shop: Lady Destrain, who hadn't been back in weeks. He tried to back out as fast as he'd come in, but the swinging door hit Delia's tail and she squealed. The lady's eyes went wide. Pol, still on the counter, stood up, yawned, and stretched. Then he arched his back and hissed at Delia, spitting as savagely as if he were about to start the cat fight to end all cat fights.

Delia snarled back.

"Dee, not in the house," he told her warningly, but the damage was done.

"Oh, dear," Lady Destrain murmured ineffectu-

121

ally. "Oh, dear, I really think—that is, I'm *sorry*, Merovice dear, but I really must—"

Twenty seconds later, the outer door was closing behind her.

"Jermyn," Merovice said dangerously.

"I'm sorry, Aunt Merry. I didn't see her," he said, hastily pulling Delia off his shoulder. He glared meaningfully at Pol, who yawned ostentatiously into his face. Delia sniffed.

"How many times do I have to tell you that that animal of yours doesn't belong in the front? She frightens the customers."

"You let her in yourself, before," he protested. "And Lady Destrain wouldn't have been scared if Pol hadn't made a fool of himself by pretending he was about to start a fight."

"How dare you say that about Pol," she said. "He knows better than to make a scene. That devil's child of yours—"

"Don't call her that!" he shouted, surprising himself with his volume. "It isn't true. She isn't a devil's child, and I won't have her called that."

Delia, taking one startled look at his face, promptly slipped out of his arms and scuttled to the rear of the shop. He sent her a brief command: *Stay there!* He had to get her out of the way—Pol was sitting up and suddenly wary, his amber eyes fixed on Merovice's face.

"It's only an Old Country name for skunk, as you well know," she said coldly. "The beast has got to learn that there are rules, and that a proper familiar obeys them. She's always causing trouble, upsetting Pol—"

"She upsets Pol? Aunt Merry, that mangy cat of yours won't leave her alone. He won't even let her sleep on her own pillow without bothering her."

"Well, he still remembers when it used to be his."

"So let him have it back," Jermyn retorted. "I told you we ought to get Delia a new one. She—"

"We can't afford extras," Merovice shot back at him. "Even the little bit of leather you bought for the girl to make that silly pad was too dear—"

He took a deep breath. "So we use an old blanket folded four times. She won't care, so long as it didn't used to be Pol's. She isn't fussy—like *some* familiars I could name."

They were fighting—but they never fought seriously. All the years—all the arguments with his aunt—Jermyn had never heard her sound like this, nor had he ever spoken to her so. He was conscious of a coldness in the pit of his stomach, but he wouldn't back down. He wouldn't! She had to realize—

"This is all her fault," Merovice said angrily. "If you'd only attached a normal familiar like a normal—"

She stopped, as if she'd just heard her own words,

and her hand went over her mouth as if to call them back.

There was a long moment of silence in the shop. Aunt and nephew glared at each other as the hurt stretched taut between them. Even Pol seemed more like a statue of a cat than a living familiar, sitting still and upright in his place on the counter.

Jermyn found his voice first. "That is enough, Aunt," he said over the throbbing in his temples. If Delia had still been in the room, he might have been even angrier—if that were possible. But she was safe in the back, hiding from the quarrel as he'd commanded. "Enough, and more than enough. I'm tired of apologizing for my familiar, more tired of apologizing for what I do and what I am. And I'm *especially* sick and tired of feeling guilty because of all you've done for me, when I never asked you to do anything at all! You and your plots to force me to awaken my magic—maybe if you'd just left well enough alone, none of this would have happened. Maybe if you'd just left *me* alone, we'd both be better off."

"Nephew, I—"

He cut her off. "*Enough*, I said!"

Grabbing his cloak, he headed out the door. Not even his aunt's calling his name could slow him down as he plunged into the wind and rain.

9

EXCURSIONS

THE RAIN came down in sheets from a dull gray sky, and the wind was colder than chilling. He could scarcely see where he was going, and didn't really care. The weather exactly matched his mood. Of course Aunt Merry was upset and of course she was under a strain—but Powers Beyond, so was he! Did she think it was easy, leaving her every day to go off and try to study magic with someone else? Didn't she realize he was studying as hard as he could so that someday *soon* he'd be able to help her? And it never seemed to go fast enough, and he never seemed to get anything right. Master Eschar was researching the curse too, but these things took time. Didn't she understand?

He slowed before a great muddy swamp in the middle of High Street, as abruptly ashamed of himself as he'd been angry a moment before. Of course Aunt Merry understood. Of course she realized. She was blaming herself, too. And he, at least, could work toward a solution to their problems. She couldn't do anything but wait.

It must be driving her crazy, he acknowledged soberly, shaking water out of his collar. *Just to sit in the shop day after day and do nothing. No wonder she's so tense.*

He almost turned around to apologize, but then thought better of it. He'd come half the distance to Temple Square already, and it might be a good idea to let Merovice have some time to think a little. *Especially since*—he squelched forward ruefully—*she hasn't had the advantage of rushing out into a freezing rain to help her temper.* He'd bring her a peace offering—flowers, maybe. Then he looked at the rain, wondering if even autumn flowers could survive this storm, and doubting it. He'd bring her something sweet and not too expensive, like candied almonds. Yes, and he'd tell her what Master Eschar said about the coin, too, and then ask her opinion.

It took him almost half an hour to slog to Wisteria Street, fighting the wind and rain every step of the way. By the time he got there, he felt like the proverbial drowned rat. Hesitantly, he rapped on the door. It was late, almost dinnertime, and Master Eschar might have gone out for the evening. If the others were in the kitchen he might have to go round the back.

But Mrs. Dundee opened the door almost at once.

"Why, Jermyn," she said, her eyes round with surprise, "what are you doing here? Little Meg said you'd gone home."

"I did," he sighed, stepping into the hall. "I came back. Is Master Eschar in his study?"

"He is—I've just taken him in his tea. Now you be careful how you scrape those boots, young man. I've no mind to be cleaning the rugs again anytime soon. Would you like some tea? There's no scones, but I've a nice tea cake, baked fresh this afternoon. And give me your cloak. If I hang it over the kitchen fire, it might be almost dry by the time you're ready to leave."

Smiling gratefully, he handed her the sopping garment. "Bless you, Mrs. Dundee. I would love some tea and cake."

In the study, Master Eschar was intent over a book, as usual. A cup of tea—rosehip, for choice—stood ignored at his elbow. He looked up when Jermyn entered, as surprised as Mrs. Dundee had been.

"Jermyn," he said, then frowned. "You certainly weren't worried when you left here. What's happened?"

Jermyn sat down with a sigh. The fire felt good. "Yes, something's happened. I don't know how serious it is, but I thought—that is, Aunt Merry said—"

Eschar's eyes narrowed. "Shall I ring for tea?"

Jermyn grinned. The Theoretician claimed that the only social response he knew was to feed people; his immediate reaction when someone brought him a personal problem was to offer refreshments. "Don't bother. Mrs. Dundee is bringing it. And I think I'd better get this out first."

"Well, get on with it, then!"

"On my way home, the Marquis of Lumiansk met me and offered me a ride in his carriage," Jermyn said baldly. "I didn't know how to refuse without giving insult, so I accepted."

Eschar's jaw tightened. "You shouldn't have. You should have been violently and embarrassingly insulting, if necessary. No standard of courtesy is worth putting you within that—that *politician's* reach."

"I found that out," Jermyn acknowledged, sighing.

"What did he do?"

"Tried to put a Persuasion on me," Jermyn said.

Eschar bit off an expletive. "To do what?"

"I'm not altogether sure," Jermyn said, his brow wrinkling. "There was the usual, I remember—"

"And that is?"

"Well, he wanted me to spy on you—what you were doing, what you were working on," Jermyn explained. "Of course, I was pretty much expecting that sort of thing—"

"Of course." Eschar was amused.

Jermyn blushed but went on doggedly. "Most of my life I've known apprentices who made some money on the side by selling information about their masters. Not very good apprentices, or good masters either, for that matter, but—well."

"Well." Eschar's eyes twinkled, but his voice was sober. "And this was something *un*expected? In what way?"

"I wish I could remember," Jermyn said, holding in a yawn. It really was very warm and comfortable in the study. If he didn't watch out, he'd doze off right in the middle of the conversation. "It all went fuzzy—he did seem to be talking about the weather, but with all the rain that might have been only natural."

"The weather," Eschar mused. "That's curious. The statistics I gave Master Douglas this morning were mostly about the weather."

"That's it!" Jermyn said, waking up again with a jerk. "The box file!"

"What?"

"One of the things I kept seeing during the Persuasion was something sort of dark colored and blocky," he explained. "Sort of squarish, but not quite. I kept feeling that I ought to know what it was, but I couldn't think of it until just now. It looked like one of the green box files that you keep important papers in, like the one you had me fetch from your desk for Master Douglas."

The Theoretician raised one eyebrow. "A curious coincidence—if indeed it is a coincidence. Do you think it was that box file, the one I gave Douglas?"

"I don't know," Jermyn said, honestly. "It could have been, I suppose. But why?"

"I've no idea." Eschar sat up straight. "It was nothing particularly vital—just raw data, and I'm not entirely certain anyone in the Guild except myself or the Spellcaster could understand much of it without help. What was the focus of the Persuasion?"

"This coin." He brought it out and laid it on the desk. Eschar studied it without touching. "Aunt Merry says it's white gold."

"It would be," he said briefly. "Hmm, standard Lumianskan currency on this side—and on the other—"

Delicately he flipped it over with the tip of a ruler. His eyebrows lifted.

"*M* and *L*," he said, surprised. "That means it's part of the Marquis's personal fortune."

"You mean, it stands for 'Marquis of Lumiansk'?" Jermyn said, blinking. "How can he mint his own coins?"

"It isn't uncommon in Continental principalities. The greater magnates have almost Royal power in their own realms," Eschar said. "The spell that's attached to this, now—I wonder . . ."

He stood up and began to pull one book after another off the bookcase, scanning briefly through each and discarding it. Jermyn watched in silence, holding in another yawn—he knew better than to speak when the Master was trying to look something up—and wished Mrs. Dundee would come in with the tea. Maybe she'd had to brew a fresh pot.

"No good," Eschar said, tossing the last book he'd opened onto his desk. "We know so little about Continental magic—"

"Sir?" Jermyn ventured. "I thought magic was illegal on the Continent."

Eschar flung himself down in his chair and absentmindedly took a swallow of cold tea. "It is, but it still exists there. We all came from the Continent once, Jermyn. The talents for sorcery were known to our ancestors in their primitive and more terrifying forms. It was only after the Emigration that we began to discover and formulate the Laws of Magic, though there are those in the lands our ancestors left who would to this day deny that wizardry knows any law."

"But—if we know what we're doing, and they don't," Jermyn said slowly, "then why can't our spells overpower theirs?"

"Oh, they can—usually. But talent is where you

find it, and the mumbo jumbo passed down from hedgewitch to hedgewitch, from black artist to child, has the force of a thousand generations of use behind it. They don't know how it works, but they know that it *does* work—usually. We can't study Continental magic because so little about it has been written down, and the priests—not ours, theirs—tend to burn what little there is as soon as they get their hands on it," Eschar finished gloomily.

Jermyn was still puzzled. "So you think that the Persuasion spell focused on the coin was Continental magic?"

"So I would assume. The Marquis wouldn't risk buying such a thing from a Guild wizard. He must have felt the need severely; Continental magic is not reliable at the best of times."

"Is that why it failed with me?" Jermyn asked.

"Probably," Eschar said. He smiled. "Oh, don't look so gloomy, boy—you've brought me a piece of a very pretty puzzle here. If the spell matrix is set into the coin itself, we may even be able to untangle it and learn from it—or send it back to the wizard who set it. No, no, this is most interesting. I'd no idea the Marquis wanted my services so badly that he'd try to suborn my apprentice. I wonder what he was thinking of? In the meantime, we'd best warn everyone in the household about offers of white gold coins from a certain nobleman. Ah, Mrs. Dundee, we were just talking about you."

"Me, sir?" She set the tray down on the little table. "Is something wrong?"

"Perhaps. Is Meg about?"

"In the hall. She helped me carry the tea things, but I thought—"

"Excellent," the Theoretician interrupted. He raised his voice. "Meggan? Come in, please."

She wore a blue pinafore, with an apron. With her hair tied up in a matching blue ribbon, she looked about twelve years old. Jermyn's mouth felt dry at the thought of her being coerced by the Marquis.

"Is something the matter, sir?" she said shyly. "If it's about that yellow china vase, I *am* sorry—"

Eschar's lips quirked into a smile, but he remained commendably grave. "I assure you, my dear, I never cared for that vase in the slightest. It had very poor lines. Please, sit down."

In quick sentences, he explained what had happened to Jermyn. Meggan looked at him in amazement as the story unfolded, but Mrs. Dundee appeared to take it in stride.

"So it's siege conditions, then," she said, nodding. "Just like the old days. Ah, me. I thought we were finished with all that."

"So did I," Eschar said.

"Has this happened before?" Jermyn asked. He tried to catch Meggan's eye, but she was looking at the floor.

"Powers, yes." Mrs. Dundee shook her head,

133

clucking. "Before the Master retired there was always someone trying to worm his way in, or find out what was what—worse before the old king died. You think they'd learn this house isn't to be taken in that way. But then, this is a new group, isn't it? These Limskis?"

"It is," Eschar said. "Meg? Do you have any questions?"

"No, sir," she said, with downcast eyes. Her face was very pale, and she twisted her hands in her apron. For once, she had nothing to say. "I—do understand."

"That's fine, then," the Theoretician said. "Now I think Jermyn could do with his tea."

Mrs. Dundee heaved herself out of her chair. "And we've the washing up to do. Come, Meggie."

Meggan followed her without a word. Jermyn watched her go, puzzled and a little hurt. She could have said something to him.

He looked up and flushed to find Master Eschar regarding him gravely.

"Sir, I—"

"Don't say anything, lad," Eschar said, smiling a bit ruefully. "I think there is something I should explain to you about our Meg. About why she is so upset."

"I didn't think—" Jermyn hesitated, warmed by the implications of "our Meg" and unwilling to say that she hadn't seemed so upset to *him*. "Is she worried it might happen to her?"

"I doubt it." Eschar dismissed the thought. "No, I'm afraid what's troubling Meggan is her parentage. She's half Lumianskan."

"What?"

"Didn't you realize? It's why she's so fair—Lumiansk tends to produce blonds. Her father was a churchman attached to the Lumianskan Embassy—their minor prelates can marry—and her mother was a former student of mine who was briefly employed in the Embassy," Eschar said briskly. "Alys died in childbirth when Meggan was small, and the baby with her. Meggan's father appointed me her guardian in case of his own death, which happened last year."

"Then—she was raised in Lumiansk?" Jermyn asked. It would explain why she found the city so strange and threatening that she rarely left the house, and never alone. And, he realized suddenly, it was probably what Aunt Merry had been referring to earlier.

"For the most part," Eschar said. "She was very ill when she came to me—from the shock of her father's death, according to the healer I consulted. She naturally doesn't like to be reminded of that period."

"Of course not," Jermyn said loyally. "I can see where it would bother her. Is that why she doesn't go out to school?"

"Yes," Eschar said, fiddling with the cold cup on his desk. "She's still so new to the city—to the whole West, in fact—that I thought it best to wait awhile.

And it isn't as though I can't tutor her myself. May I trouble you for some of that fresh tea?"

"Of course, sir." Jermyn poured in silence. "I really ought to be going home . . ."

"Yes, of course," Eschar said, sipping. "Unless you'd like to discuss what happened with your familiar this afternoon?"

"Oh, that wasn't—" Jermyn's mouth fell open. "How did you know Delia was in trouble this afternoon?"

Eschar smiled. "You're wearing the new shoulder pad, which means you must have tried it on and rushed out of the house—without your familiar, and without bothering to take the pad off. Which argues a problem. Did the pad work?"

"Yes, it did, or it seems to," Jermyn said, wondering if Meggan had told Master Eschar about their project or if he had found out some other way; he always did seem to find things out. "But that wasn't— I mean—"

"Don't struggle so, boy." Eschar sipped tea and smiled at him. "You have admitted you had trouble with your familiar, and as your apprentice-master I ought to be informed of any such. Especially if—as I suspect—the real trouble is with your aunt."

Jermyn almost choked on his tea cake. This from the man who claimed he had no skill at personal problems? "Sir, I'm grateful, but I really don't think there's anything you can do right now that you aren't already—Powers! What was that?"

That was a great crack of lightning, followed instantly by thunder. The sky blazed. The window at the front of the study blew in, scattering papers and letting in rain that lashed against the bookcases. Gasping, Jermyn jumped to fasten it and found himself struggling to simply hang on. Again the thunder boomed. And again.

"That's no natural storm," Eschar said over the rising wind, as he helped Jermyn slam the window. "Was it looking this bad when you came across the city?"

"No!" Jermyn shouted. "It was raining hard, but there wasn't any lightning."

Glare lit the western sky brighter than sunset would have if the clouds hadn't been in the way; there was another crackle of electricity, almost palpably near.

"That's far too close," Eschar said. "And this is going on far too long. We shouldn't have weather this severe in the city. What's wrong with the Weather Master?"

"Master Eschar!" Mrs. Dundee stood in the doorway, her apron twisting in her hands. Behind her, Meggan was white-faced. "Master Eschar, that lightning—the city's on fire!"

10

STORM AND FIRE

ESCHAR SNAPPED out crisp instructions, scarcely pausing as he swung his cloak over his shoulders.

"Mrs. Dundee, you and Meggan secure the house, but don't take chances. The cistern should be full—use it! Jermyn, I want you with me."

In the distance, first one fire horn, then another kicked in. The out-of-key wailing set Jermyn's teeth on edge, but Eschar merely lifted his head and listened intently.

"Catalpa District, I'd say—and that was Castle

Rising, first. It shouldn't be too bad over there. The houses are mostly stone in the west end. Ah, there's Riverbend. I thought we'd be hearing from them soon."

"Riverbend!" Jermyn gasped at the third siren. "Sir, should I—"

"You should come with me, apprentice," the Theoretician said sternly. "The Riverbend Fire Brigade turns out whenever there is a fire anywhere in the city—too much wood down dockside to take risks; you know that. Don't worry, the rain will help them."

They were out in the street, Jermyn trotting to keep up with Eschar's long stride. The rain and wind lashed his face like icy whips. He could smell the fire.

"Sir," he cried against the storm. "Sir, the fire's that way!"

"Do I look like a fire brigade?" Eschar shouted back, annoyed. "We're going to the Guild Hall, to the Spellcaster. He's the one to handle this."

When they reached the Guild Hall, Steen Douglas was already up and about, rampaging around the golden oak-paneled entrance in an incongruously elegant maroon dressing gown. He looked shaky, but his eyes were bright with worry. Standing next to him was a tall, fair-haired woman dressed in rose-colored silk. Jermyn recognized her as his aunt's friend, the healer Ardatha Collins.

Douglas didn't seem the least surprised to see Eschar.

"Wondered when you'd turn up," he said testily. "Oh, go away, woman. Do!"

"Not when I'm the only thing that's keeping you on your feet," Healer Collins snapped right back at him. She wore the look of concentration that Jermyn knew meant she was healing in some way, and the slim willow wand she held between her hands was glowing softly silver. "Without my strength to support you, you're helpless, you old fool. And the city needs you, more's the pity!"

"Yes, yes, I know," he said irritably. "Where's Fulke? We've got to get this wind to die down before the whole city goes."

Jermyn felt his stomach lurch.

"He may not be able to get through," Eschar said. "If he does, we'll put him to work. In the meanwhile, what's to be done?"

"Catalpa's safe, for now," Douglas told him. "I cast the fireshield myself. It won't last long, though. Castle Rising is upwind and at risk."

"What about Riverbend?"

"They're watching, but it's spreading in the other direction, so far. That's bad enough. We'll need a shield over the whole city, soon."

Eschar frowned. "Can you cast anything that big?"

"He cannot," Ardatha Collins put in, her concentration never wavering. "We'll have to make do with his guidance, for he has not the strength to cast magic."

"I'm still the ranking Spellcaster in this city," Douglas said, affronted. "Get me the spell and I'll make the magic stick, all right. Blast, now what?"

A great crash without, and a young man wearing a journeyman's badge on his tunic burst into the room. "Master Douglas, the Council Oak—it's been struck by lightning. It's on fire!"

"Then put it out," Douglas said. "Powers Above and Beyond, must I do everything myself?"

He raised both his hands in the direction of the rear of the Guild Hall and muttered a brief incantation. Jermyn felt the power go out of the old man like a wave. It did not flow back.

"Douglas!" Eschar cried in sudden alarm. He leaped forward, but Ardatha was before him to ease the Spellcaster to the floor.

"I told you so," she scolded.

Master Douglas grimaced weakly, clutching at his chest. "Foolishness," he murmured. "Should know better than to react like that—worry about an old tree when the city's on fire. Sorry, boy . . . looks like it's up to you."

It took Jermyn a moment to realize that Douglas was calling the Theoretician "boy."

"You'll get no more out of him this night, William," Healer Collins was saying.

"Then we will cope without him." Eschar stood up. "Even his last spellcasting might be of use to us. You—Journeyman Tevic, isn't it? Tell whatever masters are in residence that I want them in the Cloister at once."

"The—the Cloister, sir?" the journeyman said, confused.

"Yes, by the Council Oak. Who is the most experienced spellcaster we have available?"

Tevic's eyes rolled wildly at the prone figure of Master Douglas, but he answered strongly enough. "Why—I am, sir."

Eschar frowned. "A journeyman spellcaster—we can manage, I believe. Jermyn, come with me."

They left the Spellcaster lying on the floor, with Healer Collins to care for him. The covered cloister in the center of the Guild Hall was just off the Chapter House. Jermyn had never seen it, but he knew that in the center of the Cloister garden was a great oak, too large for fewer than ten men to encircle with outstretched arms. It was said that the first Council of Wizards had come to an accord under the tree, and built the first Guild Hall around it when the city was still little more than a fort in the Western wilderness.

Now the oak was on fire. It hissed in the rain as the wind whipped the flames higher. Jermyn could feel something trying to contain it, but the fire was too strong.

"Can you sense Douglas's fireshield?" Eschar asked him.

"Is that what it is? Yes, sir, there's something trying to hold the fire back. To damp it down."

"To starve it," Eschar corrected him. "Fire can't breathe without air any more than human beings can, and a fireshield cuts off the supply of air."

"Well, it's there, whatever," Jermyn said. This, he suddenly realized, was why he'd been brought along: Master Eschar, not being a practicing wizard, would have had great difficulty monitoring the state of a spell in progress. "Only, it's too weak."

"Because Douglas was. Besides, it was only a temporary shieldspell. However, we should be able to build on that framework. Ah, Croy, Caleb—any others?"

"Tenzil's coming," a short, fat master said. "And Mora said that if you need her, she'll be on the roof."

"We need her. Tevic, you know the shortest way. Run and tell Mistress Crane on the roof to prepare a bracing spell on the building. Tell her to make it one that will work without her close attention. We're going to strain the foundations tonight."

"You mean to work in concert?" the other wizard said, frowning. "That's dangerous."

"Not as dangerous as letting the fire spread unchecked," Eschar said. "Which it will, in this wind. If we can save the Council Oak, we should be able to mimic this small fireshield over the whole city—or at least the most endangered parts of it."

"Sympathetic magic," the fat man said. "With no full spellcaster, you'll need an earth wizard for that, and spellmakers are hard to come by."

"He has an earth wizard, if not a spellmaker," Healer Collins said from the Cloister entrance. She looked pale in the leaping firelight. "As a healer, I have sufficient earthmagic to serve—though I suggest you hurry, William. The fire has injured many people already, and the healing aspect of my talent will take over as soon as enough people are in pain."

"Don't let it happen," Eschar ordered her. "Now, my friends, what we are about to do is quite sound—in theory, at least."

He arranged the wizards just in front of the burning tree, in a six-pointed star rather than the usual pentangle. The latecomer, Tenzil, tried to argue, but Master Eschar stood firm: six points it was, with Croy, Caleb, and Tenzil on three of them. The wizard named Mora Crane—she turned out to be a prognosticator with some building magics—took one of the open points, while Tevic took the other. The journeyman looked yellow with fear, and Jermyn didn't blame him.

Ardatha took first point.

"Jermyn, you'll walk the circle," Master Eschar said, briskly. He had positioned himself to the left of the first point of the star, where he could see and guide the others.

"Huh?" was Jermyn's elegant response. "Me? But—"

"Yes, you. All you have to do is carry the taper around and light the candles with it. Walk in and out of the points of the star, never stepping across the lines. You can reach across them to light the candles— in fact, you must—but you must never step completely across them. Is that clear?"

Jermyn tried to re-swallow his stomach. "Yes, sir."

Eschar raised his voice. "You may begin, Ardatha."

Healer Collins didn't seem to hear him. At the top point of the star, she was outlined against the fire. She stood with her head lifted, as if she were listening for a signal. Jermyn fancied that he could see the light of the larger fire in her eyes, the fire that must not spread.

She raised her hands in a sudden, fluid motion.

"Prime," she said.

Jermyn shivered. All healers had some connection to the earthmagic, to the birth of things that preceded even the elements, but he didn't like to think about it. The Prime Mover was the first Power. Then—

"Earth," Mora said from Ardatha's right, her round face very serious. Earth was the base element,

145

first among equals. It was Earth's power that they meant to invoke tonight.

"Water," the fat wizard, Croy, responded. That was the third point and the second element.

"Air," said Caleb, on the fourth point.

Tenzil took a deep breath. "Fire," he intoned, the last element, and the one that threatened to destroy them.

The fire in the oak tree stretched upward, flames shooting as the element heard its name.

Jermyn blinked hasty tears out of his eyes; his hands trembled.

Tevic's turn—he stood opposite Prime as the last point on the star and the only other one without a separate element. He represented the Totality. Ordinarily the final point of the star was the strongest, but for controlling individual elements it was the least significant. All it required was a warm body as a conductor. Jermyn sensed Mora's reinforcement spell steadying the walls around them, and he nodded reassuringly at Master Eschar. The building would hold, but the forces they were invoking were powerful enough to bring down the whole Guild Hall if they got loose. And to be doing a Great Magic in concert without a master spellcaster—he just hoped Aunt Merry never got to hear of it.

Eschar was looking at the journeyman encouragingly, and Tevic stiffened.

"World," he intoned, in a voice that shook only a little. "Begin!"

Ardatha—Prime—answered: "First light."

Jermyn walked over to her, careful to step outside the lines of the star, and applied the taper to the candle she held so steadily. The walls sheltered them from the rain just enough for the little flame to catch. Now that the circle was closed, none of the wizards would move—indeed, they *couldn't* move. Great Magics had a tendency to freeze mere bone and muscle.

Master Eschar pointed silently, and Jermyn walked to the left and back: Earth next, for balance.

"Second light," Mora said. Jermyn touched the candlewick, and it caught reluctantly. Something inside him trembled with the flame—the power leaping upward to the sky.

Water followed, because it was fire they were trying to control. Jermyn lit the candle smoothly, hardly daring to breathe.

"Third," Croy said, his eyes glazed and his body stiff.

Now Air—to bracket Fire. Wind was Air, and Wind would feed Fire if not controlled, but Caleb was controlling it. His lips moved as he repelled the air before him, and he didn't speak at all. The fifth wizard—Fire—was less entranced. Tenzil braced himself visibly as Jermyn reached him, but held still. Jermyn held the taper to the wick.

It flared, sputtered—and, at Tenzil's urging, died to a pulsing spark.

"Quickly, Jermyn!" Eschar called.

He focused on the world candle in Tevic's hand. Careful, carefully now—it didn't take training to do this part. Any halfway competent child could do it. Aunt Merry's Pol could have done it, if he had been born with hands.

He lit the candle, and leaped back as the fire flared straight up out of the taper. Master Eschar was shouting something, but Jermyn couldn't hear what it was. He fell to his knees at the edge of the circle, feeling the ground tremble beneath him and the rain dashing against his body.

The Oak first—the Council Oak, older than the Guild Hall, almost older than the city—but an oak, just like the sprigs he'd used in his experiments . . .

Mist swirled around the great tree as fire crackled in its branches and began, reluctantly, to sputter and go out. The wind died, and the fire in the tree above them sank with it to glowing embers.

Now reach out, to the city . . .

Jermyn felt rather than saw Ardatha start to spread her tap into the source of things, into the earthmagic, reaching down into the land that was there before people had built their houses and halls on it, and spreading her reach out into all the land that was the city. He could feel the strain as she took the power into herself and sent it out again to the world, through herself. Journeyman Tevic braced himself, then sagged forward into semiconsciousness with an inarticulate moan.

Jermyn closed his eyes.

It's working. It's working. It—the tree . . .

The tree was falling! Still glowing with banked fire, it creaked ominously toward the oblivious, taut circle of wizards. It must not have been able to stand the strain, the extension of the spell that blanketed the entire city. But if it fell, it would take the circle with it, crushing the wizards. Gasping, Jermyn put out his hands as if he could lift the great trunk back upright by himself. Something—sparks? rainbows? moonlight?—arched from his fingertips, caught at the tree and held it steady. The branches stirred as if part of a conscious, aware thing. He fought to hold them still, to hold every rustling leaf in place; and choked as the power flickered. It wasn't enough. It couldn't be . . .

And then it was as if a wall went down in his mind, and all the pieces fell neatly into place. There was a calm, steadying warmth inside him, an echo.

Knew you could do it, boy, said Aunt Merry's voice in his memory. *All you needed was a little push.*

And a breathy voice in the back of his mind said: *Good Je'm'n. Very good Je'm'n.* That wasn't a memory, he realized; that was Delia! Had he called on her to help him? He must have. The power flowed strong and true through her, from where she was waiting for him across the city, as the familiar-bond put him in touch with magic itself. It was power, it was inside of him and all around him, and it was there for him to use. He did so: *Strength to the root, to the bole, to the branches—fill the empty spaces with light, and return to the flowering spring.*

The old tree shook, straightened—stayed. Its roots were intact. He realized with an odd detachment that it might even grow again.

His eyes were still closed, but that didn't matter: he could feel it now, through the circle of wizards. He was a part of the whole of magic. In the dark behind his eyelids, he could see the city like the afterimage of fire. The flames were swirling in multicolored mist, screaming out in frustration, dying. They hissed away into nothingness, into warm true darkness, into ashes. And the land itself breathed a sigh of relief.

It was working.

It had worked.

Jermyn opened his eyes to find Master Eschar an arm's length away, staring at him with a startled expression on his face.

"Jermyn," he said, so quietly that not even the circle of wizards could hear, "what in the name of all the Powers Themselves did you just *do?*"

11

AT THE WEATHER MASTER'S

HE HAD no time even to try to think of an answer
before Master Caleb interrupted them. Apparently,
neither he nor the others had noticed anything unusual.

"That was quick thinking, Eschar," Caleb said
tiredly. "How did you know this configuration?"

The Theoretician shrugged. "An old variant."

"The question is not how we did it," Tenzil said,
joining them. "The question is, what do we do now?"

Eschar's expression became even more grim.
"Now, I think I will leave you to settle matters here,

while Jermyn and I pay a call on the Weather Master."

Caleb frowned. "Yes, I can see where you might. Though usually he leaves most of the day-to-day business to his journeyman."

"So I'd heard," Eschar said, frowning. "Still, I prefer to speak to Fulke directly. The local Constabulary will need to be informed, too."

"Powers, yes," Caleb said. "I forgot all about them. They'll be wanting an explanation for so much storm magic gone wrong. The Guild liaison is named Andrews—he's the most likely to have been assigned to this."

"Middle-sized, with dark hair? I know him," Eschar said thoughtfully. "He is not entirely a fool. You'd better find a healer to tend to Ardatha, Caleb, she looks all done in. Come, Jermyn."

The streets were empty and dark; it was fortunately still raining. On the way to Fulke's formal residence, in the Weather Hall, Jermyn wondered if he should check in with Aunt Merry. He was on the point of asking, when the Theoretician spoke.

"We can be private now, Jermyn," he said, his voice quiet. "And I would like an answer to the question I asked you back there in the Cloister. If you please."

"Yes, sir," Jermyn said, all thoughts of his aunt

leaving his mind. It was almost hard to remember all the smoke and the magic now. Had he really done something that strange? "I'm not sure what I did, sir. Just, the tree was falling into the circle, and I— stopped it. Sort of."

"How?" A quiet, disembodied voice floated out of the darkness. "I have taught you no regrowth spells."

"It was a shieldspell—I think," he said. "Like the one I tried to use against Fulke that day in the Registry Courtyard. Aunt Merry taught me that one—only this time it worked."

"A shieldspell against magic worked to ward off a falling, physical object?"

"Yes, sir." He hadn't thought of it that way. "I think that's what happened."

Eschar was silent for a few more paces. "You took a terrible risk, apprentice, particularly working without the physical presence of your familiar."

"Yes, sir. I'm sorry, sir—but Delia was there, all right. Sort of. In my head. I'm pretty sure." The voice that hadn't been memory.

"I—see," the Theoretician said slowly. "The ability to access your familiar so strongly from this distance means that you are beginning to get control of your uncontrollable talent, which is all to the good. What you did in the Cloister would also seem to indicate that—well, we'll talk about it later."

Jermyn would have liked to ask questions, but they

had arrived at the Weather Hall—which was, unfortunately, empty and closed for the night. Even the living quarters were dark, and no one answered Master Eschar's knock.

"Not surprising," he said, sighing. "It appears that we will have to do this the hard way—or perhaps our next errand will find us a shortcut. Come, Jermyn."

They had passed a few constables on the way, out keeping the peace; one of them told Eschar that the Constabulary was working out of a temporary headquarters on Basin Street in Castle Rising District, that having been the area most severely affected. Eschar headed there with Jermyn in his wake.

The Constabulary's temporary headquarters turned out to be in what was normally someone's carriage house, and Inspector Andrews was there, too. Not above average height, he had brown eyes and he wore his hair as if he'd forgotten he needed to get it cut, long enough so that occasionally he had to brush it out of his eyes. He was as grimy and tired-looking as any of the fire fighters, but his eyes brightened when he saw the Theoretician.

"Eschar," he said, "I was just about to send for you."

"Oh?" The Theoretician sat down at a long table. "Not to lay a complaint against the Guild, I hope.

Oh, this is my new apprentice, Jermyn Graves. Jermyn, this is Inspector Andrew Andrews."

"How do you do," the Inspector said, absently shaking hands. He didn't seem the least self-conscious about his peculiar name. "No, of course there's been no official complaint, Theoretician. Not yet. But that storm wasn't natural—we had witchlights flickering as far away as the outer harbor. The Guild is going to have to offer an explanation—and soon—if it doesn't want to find itself formally censured. I assume that's what you're here for?"

"In a way," Eschar said. "In point of fact, Andrew, the Guild no more knows what caused this storm than you do, and wishes to learn the truth of the matter even more. Jermyn and I are planning to question Weather Master Fulke before tomorrow."

"You mean before dawn." Andrews grinned. "It's already tomorrow. What's my part in the expedition? I haven't the authority to question a Guild master—let alone a Council member."

"I want you to locate him," Eschar said. "He isn't at the Weather Hall, or in the Guild Hall proper. He could be trapped by this fire anywhere in the city, and I frankly am unwilling to hunt for him. Whereas you have all the resources of the Constabulary at your disposal."

"And can put half a hundred men in the streets on

a moment's notice," Andrews said with a broad grin. "Well, I'm game—but have you tried his house?"

"I told you, we've been to his residence and the Guild Hall."

"No, you said the Weather Hall. I know Orthas lived there, until his last illness, but Fulke has a house in Castle Rising District."

"Does he, now?" Eschar said, his eyes narrowing. "And Castle Rising was the first and hardest hit by this fire."

Andrews was elaborately casual. "That seems to be the case. Curious coincidence, isn't it?"

"It is," the Theoretician said. He stood up. "Can I assume that you do have the authority to get us through the fire lines?"

"I certainly do," Andrews said, reaching for his hat. "Shall we go?"

It was a good thing they had the Inspector with them: his say-so passed them right through the ranks of still anxious and laboring fire fighters. Even so, they had to make several detours. The flames were out, but there had been structural damage to several buildings, and some of the streets weren't safe.

Fulke's house was, or had been, a pretty little white-walled villa with a pleasant garden. Now the garden was a stinking ruin, the gazebo was a blackened skeleton, and the fountain was bone-dry and cracked from the heat. The walls of the house were stained black with smoke, but fire did not seem to have touched it. Eschar and Jermyn poked around the ruins while Andrews questioned his men.

Eschar frowned. "I would think that it has been evacuated."

Returning, Andrews shrugged. "It looks worse than it is. For one thing, the back of the house is completely untouched. There was no one home at the height of the fire, but if Fulke came back to check on the damage afterwards, he might easily have chosen to stay. The place is livable, despite this mess outside."

"A mess it certainly is," Eschar said. "Unfortunately. This was a pretty property."

Silently, Jermyn agreed that it must have been.

"Did you know it?" Andrews asked curiously.

"Oh, yes. Judge Cantreville owned it, before they disbarred him. I didn't know Fulke had purchased the place," Eschar said.

The Inspector coughed into his hand. "I thought you knew everything."

"No one knows everything, but I ought to have known *this*," the Theoretician said, his eyes cold. "Fulke shouldn't have been able to purchase this sort of estate outright, and Cantreville's widow would never have sold for less than the full market value, and in cash."

Jermyn leaned forward, listening intently.

"Yes, he has been throwing money around rather recklessly lately," said Andrews, too innocently. His eyes gleamed; clearly he felt he was scoring a point. "A new carriage, fancy clothes—some fairly sophisticated parties. Everyone assumed it was his elevation to the Council going to his head."

"They shouldn't have," Eschar responded, his voice as cold as his eyes. "*We* shouldn't have let it pass. Fulke would never have been able to afford such behavior on what he might lawfully earn."

Jermyn took one look at his master's face and whistled silently. If the Inspector had any sense, he'd back off—fast!

The Inspector apparently had all the sense he needed. Dropping the air of innocence, he said regretfully: "Well, I—we figured as much, but it wasn't our place to ask the Weather Master about his income. And he didn't seem to be stretching any civil or criminal laws, just Guild ones. Now, perhaps, we can ask a few questions."

The front door was locked. Andrews silently produced a ring of keys.

Eschar took them and smiled. "Skeleton keys, Andrew? And reinforced by magic, too. How thoughtful of you—ah, that should do it."

The front hall was empty, except for a small table with a familiar looking green box file sitting on it.

"That's the file you gave to Master Douglas!" Jermyn blurted.

"So it is." He picked it up and turned it over in his hands.

"Important?" Andrews asked.

"The seal isn't broken—no, it isn't remarkably important. Spellcaster Douglas asked me to chart some Continental weather patterns which he wanted to compare to ours. I suppose Fulke was interested, though why he should leave the file sitting on a table in his front hall is beyond me. Blast the man, where is he? *Fulke!*"

They found him in the workroom at the back of the house, curled up on the floor. His eyes were open, wide and staring, and his features contorted into a grimace of horror. One arm was stretched out in front of him, while the other was clenched close to his side.

Eschar dropped to his knees. "He's breathing, but his skin is far too warm. Fetch a healer."

Jermyn turned, but Andrews stopped him. "Right, I'm on it. I'll whistle up a constable. You stay here and do what you can to help."

"See if you can find a blanket," Eschar ordered.

"Will this do?" Jermyn asked. It was the purple cloak Fulke had worn on the day of the Registry encounter, still smelling faintly of fish.

"Admirably." Eschar wrapped the cloak over the

159

comatose weather wizard, and lifted the stiff form gently to tuck it around him. "What's this?"

Jermyn bent over to see: under Fulke's body, about where his left hand had been, was a white gold coin, inscribed with an *M* and an *L*.

"The Marquis!"

"Illogical," Eschar said. "He'd bought Fulke's services, after all. The last thing he'd want would be an ailing and useless employee."

"Maybe Fulke thought better of it," Jermyn insisted. "Well, there was this storm, wasn't there? Maybe Fulke finally decided he had to control it, and the Marquis didn't want him to."

Eschar shook his head, turning the coin in his hands. "Why? Burning the capital city would hardly destroy the empire, even if that is what the Lumianskans wish. Besides, it seems a bit too obvious for our friend Devereux. Incapacitating the Weather Master during the season of autumn storms is an unnecessarily wholesale and flamboyant way of announcing an attack. Anyone who has lived in the city as long as the Marquis should definitely have known better. And why pay Fulke in the first place, if that was what he had in mind?"

"Maybe it wasn't an attack," Jermyn suggested. "Maybe Fulke just happened to get sick at the wrong moment, when he was doing something for the Marquis."

"That's possible," Eschar said, his eyes straying back to Fulke. "Still, I don't know . . . we need more data."

"What's wrong with him, anyway?" Jermyn asked. "Fulke, I mean. Can you tell?"

"Fever of some sort, but not one familiar to me. It must have come on him suddenly too, or he wouldn't have crumpled here in his workroom." Eschar's eyebrows drew together in a sudden frown. "And that means—is his familiar around?"

"Yes, in the cage there." The great snowy owl was lying on its back on the bottom of an open gilded cage, both claws extended stiffly upward, and breathing shallowly. "I don't think it's in any better shape than Fulke is."

The Theoretician stood up and walked over to the cage. He looked down on the owl for a long minute, and when he turned back to the room again his face was carefully blank. "Poor bird. I was afraid of that."

"Afraid of what?" Jermyn asked, puzzled. "Wasn't it just the shock of his master's collapse?"

"Unlikely, under the circumstances." The Theoretician took a deep breath and looked directly at Jermyn. "One of the characteristics of a magic-inspired illness is that it affects not only the sorcerer so attacked, but also all those connected to him by lines of magic. The strength of the familiar-bond would insist that Fulke's familiar succumb when he did.

If Fulke's fever were natural, the owl should still be aware. Ergo, Fulke's fever and coma are not natural."

Jermyn was suddenly cold. "But—a curse is a connection between the wizard and the subject. Especially an active curse. Isn't it?"

Eschar put a sympathetic hand on his shoulder. "Yes, it is. But we can't be certain that—"

Jermyn could feel his heart hammering wildly. "Fulke cursed Aunt Merry, and she—"

"Jermyn!" He heard Eschar call him, but nothing could have stopped Jermyn now. Even bowling over Inspector Andrews in the hallway scarcely slowed him down. He had to get back to Riverbend. He had to get to the shop. He knew he should have gone home before now, should have insisted on going home after the business at the Guild Hall. The dark, storm-filled sky was breaking up into a dull, overcast sunrise, but Jermyn had no eyes to spare for the new day. He ran until he felt his lungs were on fire, hurdling barriers and neatly evading both constables and fire fighters who tried to stop him. He ran until he was running down Thornapple Lane to his own front door and came to a stumbling halt before the demurely shuttered shop windows.

Gasping for breath, he leaned against the door for half a second, then rang the bell. Twice. No answer. *Well, she might be upstairs. It is early*, he thought. Frantically he fumbled for his key. His hands trembled as he fitted it into the lock.

"Aunt Merovice, are you here?"

No one in the front—of course not, the shop was closed. The back room was hung with bags of drying herbs, but it was just as empty. He took the stairs two at a time: she was probably making breakfast, and he'd get a scolding for having been out all night, and why hadn't he at least found time to send a message?

But the kitchen was empty, too. Delia was curled in the corner by the stove, fast asleep, but of Merovice there was no sign. *So she's still sleeping.* Cautiously he eased open the door to her room and peered in: *yes, there she is.* Everything was all right. She was just peacefully asleep on the narrow cot that had been hers for as long as he could remember, with Pol cuddled by her side. For a moment, he sagged backward as relief overwhelmed him.

You moron, you might have known she'd be fine. You can't keep Merovice Graves down.

And then he noticed that she was as pale as the pillow she was lying against, and that she was barely breathing.

"Aunt Merry!"

He shook her once, twice, but she wouldn't wake up. Her skin was dry, but hot to the touch; she was deeply unconscious and burning with fever. Whatever was wrong with Fulke had taken her as well, through the curse he'd put on her. The curse she had risked for her nephew's sake.

Jermyn was sitting on the floor by the cot, clutching his aunt's hand, when Delia crawled sleepily into the room and hauled herself into his lap.

Je'm'n?

"Dee," he whispered, and buried his face in her fur. "Oh, Dee."

Aunt Merry.

12

PLAGUE

HE WAS still sitting on the floor with Delia in his lap when Eschar and the Inspector caught up with him. They held a whispered conference on the stairs, and then the Inspector went away.

Master Eschar touched his shoulder. "I'm sorry, Jermyn. You can't know how sorry I am."

"It isn't fair," Jermyn said, wondering why he wasn't crying. "It's all my fault."

"I've sent Andrews for a carriage," the Theoretician said. "We'll take her home with us. Mrs. Dundee is an excellent nurse."

"But Pol will have to come, too. And Delia, I can't leave her."

"I am aware of that," Eschar told him. "Don't worry—my rule against familiars in the house was not meant for extraordinary circumstances."

Deedee come too? Her bright, pleased black eyes comforted Jermyn. At least she could be happy about something.

He almost broke down when, in the course of packing up a few necessities, he noticed that Pol's old pillow had been replaced in Delia's corner with a shabby black and white quilt, folded four times. He knelt on the floor next to the thing, while Delia climbed into it and showed him how the folds could be pulled this way and that into a comfortably skunk-shaped nest. So Aunt Merry had listened to him after all, had tried to make amends in her own way. And now she was sick and he couldn't even thank her, or apologize. His hands trembled as he stuffed the quilt into a satchel.

The slow, careful journey through the smoke-stained streets of the city was not one that Jermyn ever cared to remember. He sat in the open wagon, next to his aunt, while Master Eschar rode on the box with Inspector Andrews. He supposed the numb coldness he was feeling was shock; in a way, he welcomed it.

Occasionally he caught snatches of conversation.

"Not certain what the prognosis . . . magical illness, has to be . . . depends on what . . . have to wait and see . . ."

At one point, Master Eschar looked back at Jermyn and said firmly: "You're quite right. I'll tell him. Later."

They were talking about him, Jermyn realized. He'd lived and worked with his aunt; if she were ill of any sort of magical contagion, through Fulke's curse, then he might very well be next. It came to him then, the risk that Master Eschar was taking, bringing Aunt Merry into his house. He supposed he should be grateful, but it was hard to care very much about anything. He set his teeth against the chill inside of him, and concentrated on keeping Delia steady on his knees. She, at least, was thoroughly enjoying the ride. Head up, she peered over the sides of the wagon with undisguised enjoyment.

They found the house on Wisteria Street in a state of controlled chaos. Meggan's eyes sparkled with excitement, but she sobered at once. Mrs. Dundee took charge immediately.

"Now, then, master, I'll send for the healer, and we'll set things to right soonest. Ah, lad, don't look so. We tough old birds are hard to kill. You'll be wanting breakfast, gentlemen. I've it all laid on in the study. Meg, come with me, please."

Meggan lingered briefly in the hall.

"Jermyn, I'm so sorry," she said, holding out her hand to him.

He took it and held on tightly. "Meg, I—I can't—"

"Everything will be all right," she said warmly, returning the pressure slightly before withdrawing. "Try to eat something. You'll feel better."

Jermyn had never felt less hungry in his life, but when he tried to follow the constables carrying his aunt upstairs, Master Eschar stopped him.

"In here, Jermyn," he said, indicating the study door. "And bring your familiar, too."

"But my aunt—"

"She'll be well cared for, and right now we need you. Trying to question a wizard's familiar without the wizard's conscious cooperation is always a difficult process."

Jermyn had set Delia down in the hallway. As he stumbled into the study, she pawed at his leg and he automatically bent to pick her up. In the study, she curled contentedly on his lap and eyed the soft-boiled eggs on the breakfast tray with interest.

Inspector Andrews handed him a cup of very dark tea, which he gulped gratefully.

"I'm sorry about your aunt, lad," the Inspector said. "And sorry to bother you now, too. I'll let you be just as soon as I've heard your familiar's story."

"My familiar's story—but what can Dee tell you?"

Eschar buttered a piece of toast and then set it down without tasting it. "Your little friend appears to be the only conscious witness to an attack of this scourge. We would like to know what happened."

"I thought Aunt Merovice was affected because Fulke was," Jermyn said, confused. "Delia wouldn't know anything about what happened to Fulke."

"But your aunt would have been affected *as* Fulke was," the Inspector said. "Perhaps in the very same instant. Anything the little skunk may have noticed could be a clue."

"If we ask her now, that is," Eschar finished. "However enhanced by magic the abilities of familiars might be, they remain only extraordinarily intelligent animals. If we—meaning you—don't ask her now, she will soon forget."

"What do you want me to ask?" Jermyn said, gently stroking Delia's back. She purred, leaning into his caress, and suggestively pointing her nose at breakfast.

"What she saw, what she heard or sensed." Andrews plainly didn't have much hope.

"Any hint of anything out of the ordinary," Eschar said briskly. He reached across the desk and offered a corner of toast to Delia. She accepted it delicately.

"I'll try," Jermyn said.

He closed his eyes to concentrate. *Delia? Deedee?*

Here, Je'm'n, she responded willingly. Absurdly, her mind-voice sounded muffled, as if she were speaking aloud around the mouthful of toast.

He waited until she swallowed and he had her full attention. *Do you remember when Aunt Merovice fell down?*

A quick, vivid image of Merovice tripping on a cake of soap he'd carelessly left in the middle of the half-scrubbed kitchen floor.

No, not that time. Last night.

Confusion. Merovice didn't fall down? Oh, of course, she must have been in bed when the spell hit. Well, Pol, then. He would have been up and about.

No response. Wait—a picture of Pol snarling and leaping into the bedroom.

Yes, that's it. What happened then?

Delia pondered, and thoughtfully chewed another mouthful of toast. If it was important to Jermyn, she was clearly willing to try. But there didn't seem to be much for her to remember. She'd looked up drowsily at Pol's departure, not much interested, and then gone back to sleep.

"Did you see any lights?" he asked desperately, aloud for Master Eschar's benefit. "Did anyone come? Did you *sense* anything at all?"

More confusion: darkness.

"Ask her what she scented," Eschar ordered, quietly so as not to disturb the rapport. "Skunks have a keen sense of smell."

Dee? Did you smell anything in the night?

A rush of understanding, pleasure at having an answer. *Oh. That. Funny smell.*

"What sort of funny smell?" he asked, and received the equivalent of a mental shrug.

Funny smell. She thought it over for a moment. *Bad.*

And that was the best she could manage, no matter how they tried: the smell had been funny and bad, and she had never smelled anything like it before.

"Then how did you know it was bad?" he asked, almost angrily.

Bad smell, she faltered. *Sorry, Je'm'n. Sorry-sorry.*

"Don't push her," Master Eschar said, when Jermyn would have persisted.

"But—"

"She can't help not being able to answer. Were she—and you—older, more experienced in your partnership, you might be able to understand her better. As it stands, you will only strain the bond."

"A bad smell, eh?" Andrews said thoughtfully. "Funny—well, funny-peculiar, to think of a skunk complaining about a bad smell."

"She isn't exactly complaining," Jermyn said, frustrated. "She's more just sort of recognizing it as bad. Oh, calm down, you silly creature. You know I love you."

He said it completely without self-consciousness; Delia was trying to crawl up his shirtfront under his tunic. He settled her back down in his lap, scratched her under the chin, and fed her another piece of toast.

Andrews was still thinking over the response. "So the odor was unfamiliar to her—and she'd know man-smell all right, even if she didn't know the person involved. Which means that most likely no one came into the shop that night."

"I doubt that there was anyone at Fulke's house either," Eschar put in. "More probably the scent was magic-borne, or at least magic-related. If I'm right about this illness, it will spread not by physical contact but by magical."

"Sir?" Jermyn ventured. "What do you think it is?"

His master moodily regarded his teacup. "I hope I'm wrong, but it has all the earmarks of a sorcerer's plague."

"What's that?" Jermyn asked.

"An archaic term for a magical contagion," the Theoretician said. "The best reference in Heliogabalus, which is—"

"Which is entirely too arcane a reference for most people, Master Eschar," Andrews said, cutting him off firmly. "If you'd explain to the boy in layman's terms, I might be able to use the same explanation to my commander."

Eschar looked affronted. "You should know as

well as I do how to research—oh, all right. A sorcerer's plague is an emotional contagion. Magic is essentially a matter of emotion, after all, of will and desire. The plague is set in a matrix, usually a fairly plain and easily transferable spell-matrix which can be implanted into a given sorcerer, often by simple exposure to its image. That sorcerer then passes on the matrix to any wizard with whom he is in psychic contact, and so on. Eventually something triggers the matrix, and that is that."

"What triggers the matrix?" Jermyn asked, frowning. "And what sets it?"

"That's the difficult part, lad," Eschar said, sighing again. "The victim's own emotional response to something—usually something quite unrelated to the plague—is the trigger. The matrix might remain dormant for days, even weeks, until the victim feels some strong emotion while going about his or her daily business. The emotion will then activate the spell, and the victim becomes ill. As for what sets the matrix in nature—nothing. It must be created."

"In other words, a sorcerer's plague is a man-made disease," Andrews said calmly—too calmly, Jermyn thought. "I admit, that still sounds a bit farfetched to me."

"It has to be deliberately created and spread—at least at first," Eschar assured him soberly. "And it can require a spellcaster of near-master strength to cast the original spell and begin the cycle of contagion. The problem is, once the cycle is begun, it can easily get out of control. Heliogabalus discusses an Eastern tribe that tried to use a plague matrix as a weapon. They wiped out their enemies all right, but then the weapon turned on them, and they couldn't stop it. They all died, to a man."

"Nasty," Andrews said, while Jermyn tried to comprehend the scope of such a disaster. "Still, *we* should be able to stop it, shouldn't we?"

"That depends," Eschar said. "If we can find the plague wizard, we can unravel the disease easily enough. In fact, just finding and breaking the spell-matrix should stop the contagion. But finding the matrix *or* the wizard may prove more than a little difficult."

"The Marquis of Lumiansk," Jermyn said into the little pause.

"What? Oh yes," Eschar said. "I don't know."

Andrews was even more doubtful. "You mean Devereux? He's no wizard."

"He employs wizards," Jermyn argued. "And we found his coin under Fulke."

"It's certainly worth investigating," Eschar said. "If nothing else, I would be interested to know just how many Guild members have accepted retainers from the Marquis."

"And that means I had better get to work," Andrews said. "I'll keep you informed, Eschar. From what you've told me, we're going to need all the help that the Guild can give us."

"Perhaps," the Theoretician said. "But I have a feeling the greatest need will be the other way around."

13

STALKING THE PLAGUE WIZARD

THE NEXT THREE DAYS were a series of night-
mares. Jermyn spent as much of his time as he could
by his aunt's bedside, just watching. ("Be careful,
Jermyn," Master Eschar warned him the first day.
"Don't get too close. Let Mrs. Dundee tend to the
nursing: she knows what she's doing.") Merovice
looked so small and frail in the big double bed, not
at all the indomitable personality she was when awake.
Unconscious, Pol lay beside her, curled into an un-
natural sleep on the extra pillow. Jermyn reached

down more than once to smooth the cat's marmalade-colored fur.

Sorry, Pol. Sorry I wasn't around to help. Sorry for everything.

The rest of the time he spent with Master Eschar, helping with his research and trying to remind him to rest and eat. Not that anyone in the city had much time to rest. Fulke and his owl were being cared for in the Hall of Healing, along with too many others. The sorcerer's plague was spreading faster than the fire had.

Steen Douglas was one of the first wizards to become ill.

"At his age, I suppose it isn't surprising," Inspector Andrews said when he brought the news.

"Due to his age, he would be very vulnerable to any magic-borne infection," Eschar agreed tiredly. "I wish it were otherwise. We need him."

The worst blow was that, contrary to all the laws of magic, healers were not immune. Ardatha Collins contracted the plague during her treatment of Master Douglas.

"But that's ridiculous!" Andrews said, when Master Eschar had summoned him in turn to tell him the news. "Healers never catch diseases from their patients. From other people, yes, but not people they are trying to heal."

"That's what I said, when Caleb first brought me

word," the Theoretician said soberly. "However, there is some evidence that healers are particularly susceptible to this sort of contagion. Their art is primarily empathy, after all, and this disease thrives on emotional contact. Mistress Collins is probably just the first of many healers to be infected."

By the second day, word had come that Master Caleb was also ill of the disease, as were the other members of their fire circle. By the third day, the Guild had declared the city under magical quarantine: no wizard, apprentice, journeyman, or master could enter or leave.

"It ought to have been done two days ago," Master Eschar growled to Jermyn in his study. "The sooner we quarantine ourselves, the better chance we have of containing this thing. The city can cope without basic services for a while, but I'm not certain the Empire itself could survive an epidemic."

"How many are ill, sir?" Jermyn asked quietly.

Eschar sighed. "Almost every weather wizard in the city. They didn't have much chance, with their craft-master stricken. No wonder the weather went berserk. Most of the healers are down as well. Those who practice the growing arts are also hard hit. So far, the healthiest are magic-workers most removed from emotional content—the spellcasters and the makers, and so on."

"What about non-magicians?" Jermyn asked, pouring Eschar a cup of tea and setting it near his hand. "Are they in danger yet?"

"Not yet," Eschar said significantly. "However, everyone living has at least a touch of psychic awareness, and it won't be long before we start hearing of cases in the general populace. I don't like to think of the panic that will cause."

Jermyn didn't like to think of it either. He was glad, now, that Master Eschar had thought to bar Meggan from Aunt Merry's room.

Meggan had not been pleased, though.

"I don't see why I can't help," she'd said rebelliously. "Mrs. Dundee's just as likely to get ill, and I'm younger and stronger than she is . . ."

Eschar shook his head. "You *can* help, child. Just stay out of the sickroom."

In consequence, Meggan ran the household while Mrs. Dundee nursed Aunt Merry. She didn't market, but she did almost everything else. And if the bacon was a little burnt on occasion, Master Eschar was too busy to comment on what he was eating and Jermyn was usually not very hungry anyway. Nor did anyone mention the dishes she broke. Who cared about a few broken plates and glasses? Not Jermyn.

He came down from sitting with his aunt on the morning of the fourth day—more accurately, Mrs. Dundee had forcibly removed him from his aunt's room and told him to go get some rest—and was desultorily tidying the study when Meg came in with a tray in her hands.

"There, I thought I heard you," she said in triumph.

Delia, who had been uneasily watching Jermyn work from her perch on a chairback, perked up at the scent of food.

"Where's Master Eschar?" he asked, sitting down at the little table. He hoped the Theoretician was catching some much-needed sleep.

"He went out early," Meggan said. She frowned. "That Inspector came for him—something about the Lumianskan Embassy."

"It must be important, then," he said, slipping Delia a piece of bacon.

"I don't—oh, there's the front door." She shook out her skirts energetically. "I'll get it. Now, don't you go feeding that animal your whole breakfast while my back is turned. She eats plenty of her own food."

Delia almost winked at him, and daintily accepted another piece of bacon.

Meggan was back in a few moments, looking irritated.

"There's a journeyman wizard at the door who won't come in," she reported. "He just stands there saying he has to see Master Eschar. Maybe you can convince him the master isn't home."

Jermyn abandoned his breakfast to Delia. He

hadn't the slightest idea who might be waiting, but he certainly wasn't expecting the person he saw standing uneasily on the front stoop.

"Peter!" he said, amazed. "What are you doing here? Why won't you come in?"

"I need to see the Theoretician," Journeyman Quail said arrogantly. He was wearing a full cloak wrapped tightly about him against the gray, cold day, and he still shivered as if chilled. His red hair was covered by a loose hood, and his face was so pale that Jermyn could see each freckle. "*Jermyn?* Why are *you* still here?"

"Where else would I be? I'm Master Eschar's apprentice."

"But you—you—" Peter stepped back and pulled his cloak in front of his face. "Are you lunatic? There's plague in this house."

"I know that," Jermyn said sharply. "It's Aunt Merry who is ill—thanks to your Master Fulke's curse."

"Your aunt?" Peter's voice almost cracked. "But then you—you're already contaminated."

Jermyn repressed a stab of pure fury, suddenly glad Delia had stayed in the study. Beside him, he heard Meggan's quick intake of breath.

"Well, obviously I'm not sick yet," he pointed out coldly. "What do you want? Master Eschar isn't home, but I suppose you could come in and wait."

"No!" Peter said, shrinking away. He seemed to recollect himself. "I—I have a responsibility. I may be the last healthy weather wizard in the city."

"Poor city," Meggan said pertly. Jermyn shook his head at her. It really wasn't funny.

"You're lucky, Peter," he said heavily. "After all, Fulke was your own master. Surely you'd been working magic with him—oh. I forgot. You've been in isolation lately."

"Why?" Meggan asked, looking from one to the other.

Peter flushed a dull beet-purple.

Jermyn grinned at her. Peter's disagreement with Delia and its consequences seemed wholly funny in retrospect. "Tell you later. Look, Peter, if you won't come in, what do you want?"

What Peter Quail clearly wanted was to stop breathing the same air as Jermyn Graves as soon as possible. He dithered a moment, and then came to a decision.

"Here," he said, pulling a green box file out from under his cloak. "This is Eschar's. You'll have to sign for it."

Jermyn eyed it. "That's the file Master Eschar gave to the Spellcaster. How did you—oh, for pity's sake, Peter, I don't bite. Why not just—"

Jaw clenched like a man on the edge of a precipice, the journeyman weather wizard leaned forward and set the file down on the stoop. "There," he said. "Now you sign for it and lay the paper down again."

"I'll do no such thing—oh, all right, all right, if you insist." Hastily Jermyn scrawled his name and set the paper down. "There. Now you can—"

The scrap of paper whisked away in the wind, and Quail gave chase. Jermyn looked after him, still grinning.

"Now *that* is a fool," Meggan said precisely, as he carried the file back into the study. "What's in the box?"

"Just some weather statistics," Jermyn said, putting it down on the table next to his breakfast. "We found it at Fulke's the morning after the fire. I suppose someone must have been cleaning up at Fulke's and noticed the master's name on the box."

"They could have picked a braver messenger."

"Oh, I don't know," he said absently. "They're probably pretty short of people over at the Weather Hall."

"Jermyn, what did he mean, you're contaminated?"

He turned to look at her. She was staring at him, her deep brown eyes full of apprehension. She twisted a single golden strand of hair nervously between her fingers.

"It's my aunt, Meg," he said gently. "Didn't you realize? The plague is infectious, and Aunt Merry and

I are connected through magic because I was her apprentice—and by blood because I'm her nephew. Sooner or later, I'm bound to come down sick, too."

"Is that why Master Eschar lets you in the sick-room but not me?" she asked. "He's afraid I'll be—infected, but he—he thinks you're already—"

"Partly that's why, I suppose," he said, and took her hands in both of his. "And probably also, he knows I wouldn't stay away from Aunt Merry even if he ordered me to. Besides, there's no reason for you to risk going into the sickroom."

Her face was very pale. "I—I didn't know. I didn't *realize*—"

"No reason why you should," he told her. "I do know that he isn't really worried about you, or Mrs. Dundee—she's a trained nurse, for one thing, and neither of you has any magical talent to let the plague take hold, for another. You should be safe with just ordinary precautions."

It wasn't the whole truth, but it would do for now, especially since Meggan was so upset. She clutched at him anxiously, leaning forward. "Jermyn, you—you can't get sick."

He smiled at her. "Well, I haven't yet. That's a good sign."

"It's not good enough," she insisted, clutching tighter. "You've got to promise me you won't get sick."

"All right, I will," he said compassionately. "I promise. Let go, Meg, you're upsetting Delia. See?"

The little skunk was on the chair, with her forepaws resting on the table. Her mouth full of egg, she looked from one to the other of them speculatively. Blushing, Meggan dropped her arms.

"I'm sorry. I—I didn't mean—"

"It's all right," Jermyn said, touching her lightly on one cheek. "Everything will be all right."

They stood for a moment very close to each other, in silence, and then Meggan turned away. As if she meant to break the mood, Jermyn thought to himself.

She turned back to the box file sitting innocently on the desk. "What should we do with this?" she asked.

Jermyn shrugged. "Master Eschar said it wasn't important. Here, let's look and see if we can sort what's in it for him."

He pulled the box over and opened it. Inside, there was a jumble of folded charts and scrawled papers.

"Is it all there?" Meggan asked anxiously. "Maybe you'd better not look too closely."

"Then how could I tell what was there and what wasn't?" he asked reasonably. "I'm not sure, but it feels just as heavy as it did the last time I picked it up. Oh, no you don't, Deedee—there's nothing for you in this box."

His familiar had climbed awkwardly from the chair

onto the table, and was poking her pointed nose into the file. She chortled at the rustle of papers, placed both forepaws on the side of the box, and pushed.

"Dee! Now look what you've done!"

The file tilted on the edge of the table, and Jermyn made a wild grab to keep it from falling over. As he did, the papers slanted forward and he caught them with his free hand.

Suddenly, there was a rush of power in the room, with the acrid scent of old magic, and a spectral *ML*, elaborately intertwined, etched itself into the air over the open box. Delia squealed and sat back on her hind legs. Meggan gasped. "What's that?" she cried.

"I don't know!" Shaken, Jermyn closed the box and opened it again; the sign was fainter but still there. "It looks like the initials on that white gold coin the Marquis tried to enchant me with. Remember?"

"Of course I remember," she said sturdily. "But Blaine Devereux couldn't have had anything to do with this file. Could he? You said it was at Fulke's."

"And Fulke was on retainer to the Marquis," Jermyn said slowly. "I don't know, Meg. But what else could this mean?"

"Well, Master Eschar will know what to do," she said, and gasped again. "I forgot—he was going to the Lumianskan Embassy. Do you think he knows about this?"

Jermyn looked at her in alarm, and closed the box

again with a snap. Delia squeaked that he'd almost caught her nose in the lid; he caressed her in quick apology. "I don't see how he can. He's scarcely left the house since the fire, and he didn't have time to examine the file then."

"We've got to tell him, then," she said firmly. "We've got to warn him."

Jermyn blinked. "We? But—you don't like to go out. Even now—"

She tossed her head impatiently. "You don't know Lumianskans. I do. *And* I know how to get to the Lumianskan Embassy."

"Isn't it on Diplomatic Row?"

"No," she said smugly. "It isn't. Now, are we going or aren't we?"

"Are you sure you want to come?"

Her gaze was steady. "I'm sure."

"Then we go," he said, standing. Delia half raised her tail—she looked worried, and he reached down to rub her gently under the chin. "We'll *all* go, all three of us. Better wear a heavy cloak, and boots if you've got some. The weather looks pretty miserable outside."

14

CONSPIRACY

THE LUMIANSKAN EMBASSY turned out to be
over by the City Gardens, and Jermyn had to admit
that he wouldn't have found it as quickly on his own.
Meggan kept her hand on his arm as they made their
way through the muddy streets; Delia's presence on
his opposite shoulder didn't deter her in the slightest.

"I don't see why you had to bring *her*," she remarked, glancing sideways at his familiar. "Or why
we didn't bring the file."

Jermyn set his jaw stubbornly; they had already
had this out before leaving the house. "I brought Dee

because she's my familiar and she is supposed to come with me. We left the file at home because we're just going to tell Master Eschar about it, not show it to him. We don't know what sort of magical safeguards Devereux set on the thing."

"How could *he* set magical safeguards on it?" she said. "He's no wizard."

"We know he's hired wizards," Jermyn said. "That's enough."

The street was a distraction. Clinging to the safety of his arm, Meggan regarded it all with wondering eyes. As usual, she had to talk about it.

"Oh, the buildings are so pretty!" she marveled. "What's that one?"

"The grain market," he told her, amused.

"No, really? It looks so impressive."

"Well, it used to be the Hall of Justice, but that's been moved. Meg, watch out—your cloak is trailing in the mud."

"I'm sorry." She pulled the black wool behind her with her free hand. "It's long, but it's the warmest I could find."

"It looks like a man's cloak," he told her. "Here, let me tie it up for you. Is it an old one of Master Eschar's?"

"No. My father's. Don't waste time, Jermyn. We're almost there."

The imposing rose and white building that served

as the Lumianskan Embassy was shuttered against the rain. There were no constables in sight, no official wagon waiting. There wasn't even a hack.

"Are you sure he's here?" Jermyn asked. "We could have missed him."

"He left the house not half an hour before you came down," Meggan said. "He must be here."

Before he could stop her, she was up the white marble steps and pounding enthusiastically on the door knocker.

"Are you crazy?" he hissed at her. "We can't just go in the front door!"

"Why not?" she said, shaking her golden hair free of her hood. "We're just going to ask if Master Eschar is within, and if he is may we wait for him somewhere out of the wet."

"*Meggan—*"

The great door swung open in front of her, and Inspector Andrews stood in the doorway glaring down at them.

"What the devil?" he said, low-voiced.

Jermyn blushed. "I—we—"

"We've come to see Master Eschar," Meggan said in her sweet, clear voice. "It's urgent."

"What could be—no, never mind," Andrews said, and hustled them both inside. "You're here now."

"Andrews? Where are you?" Eschar's voice sounded annoyed. Jermyn winced, and Delia snuffled nervously at his ear. Then the Theoretician came into the front hallway and saw them. "What are you two doing here?"

That made Meggan turn shy at last. "We—we found out something important," she said. "That is, Jermyn—I mean—"

She faltered, and Jermyn took a deep breath. "Journeyman Quail brought over that box file we found at Fulke's, right after you left, sir. We looked at it, and it manifested a sign—the initials *M* and *L*, just like on the Marquis's coin. We—we thought you'd want to know."

"We came to warn you," Meggan said in a rush. "I told Jermyn you were coming to the Embassy, and we thought—"

"You thought I might be walking into a trap," he said, still annoyed. "I assure you both, I have been taking care of myself for a good many years now, and I know what I'm doing."

"Yes, sir," Meggan said humbly. Jermyn just nodded.

"What do we do with them?" Andrews asked, looking anxiously up the stairway. "There isn't time to send them away, or anywhere to put them around here."

"We'll have to make the best of it," Eschar said, resignedly. "Into the library—quickly, both of you! Get behind the window screen and don't make any more noise than you can absolutely help."

For the first time, Jermyn noticed that Master Eschar was keeping his voice low and Inspector Andrews was too, and that both men seemed tense. And surely an embassy ought to have servants or someone to answer the door. Where was everyone?

He knew better than to ask. The long book-lined room that Master Eschar called the library had a fire burning in the hearth at one end and tall windows which let in as much of the autumn light as was available. The inner walls were lined with books—the bindings were leather, and all matched, but none of the books looked particularly well read. Against the windows, fortunately at the same end of the room as the fire, was a tall screen painted with dragons flying over snowcapped mountains. He and Meggan huddled behind the screen gratefully, leaning into the warmth of the fire. Master Eschar walked over to a desk in front of the fire and to the left of the screen. He bent over what looked like an official proclamation of some sort. With a silver eyeglass, he studied the ornate lettering absently, but Jermyn had the feeling that he wasn't seeing a thing he looked at.

Meggan recovered quickly. "What do you think—"

"Shh!" Jermyn said.

"But I was just—"

Firmly, he put a hand over her mouth and held it there until he was satisfied that he had glared her into silence. She glared right back when he took his hand away. In the back of his mind Delia snickered at him, but she kept her comments inaudible.

They could see the room from where they sat, but the screen was angled so that no one entering could see them unless he looked carefully. When the Marquis entered from a side door, he was not looking carefully. He had two great wolfhounds with him, on leads, their heads reaching above his waist. The dogs were dry, unlike Delia who was dripping all down Jermyn's shoulder.

The Lumianskan stopped short.

"Master Eschar," he said guardedly. He took a firmer grip on both dogs, shortening their leads. "Tracer, Greatheart. Stand. Watch."

The dogs froze, the commands clearly focusing their attention on Master Eschar, who smiled.

"Marquis," he responded, nodding graciously.

"I had been given to understand that you left the Embassy some time ago, with the—er—Constabulary contingent," the Marquis said. "To what do I owe the honor of this further visit?"

"Oh, I came back after Inspector Andrews and his men went home," Eschar said vaguely. "I admit, I was surprised to find that you had gone out again, good princeling."

The Marquis smiled. "So, the charade is finished, is it? Well, I did not think that so stressing my father's name and house would conceal my mother's heritage forever. And there is no law that says Lumiansk's representative to the Empire cannot also be a member of her Royal House on his mother's side."

"No law indeed," Eschar said, sounding pleased. "Still, I find I am relieved to have solved the puzzle of why you preferred your father's name to your title. I had wondered. It makes sense that you might try to obscure your royal connections a trifle, if you had— plans. But there is also no law against Lumiansk's representative using what name he chooses. Provided that he *is* the duly selected representative of the Imperial Governor of Lumiansk, of course."

One of the wolfhounds whined. Its mate pulled on the leash and began to whiffle the air nervously. Behind the screen, Delia preened herself in a self-satisfied manner. Jermyn took a fresh grip on her and shook his head warningly at Meggan, who crossed her eyes and stuck out her tongue at him.

"Of course," the Marquis said sleekly. "As I am."

"Considering the probable condition of the current Imperial Governor, I imagine that you are," Eschar agreed. "I won't bother to ask how you managed to ensorcell him—because I don't need to ask. I can find out easily enough, if I wish. Someone should have warned you about Persuasions, Devereux. They always leave a mark."

The Lumianskan's eyes narrowed. "You have no proof."

"I don't need proof," Eschar said regally. "All I have to do is summon Inspector Andrews again and denounce you to him, and you will be recalled. Unless . . ."

The Marquis's face relaxed slightly. "Unless what?"

"Why, my dear Devereux, how forgetful you are," Eschar almost purred. "You have several times offered me your prince's retainer."

"Which you have several times refused."

"I do not deal in paltry sums."

Behind the screen, Meggan uttered an all but inaudible outraged gasp. The female wolfhound looked their way and whined again. Her mate stretched his leash toward the screened end of the room and uttered one sharp, short bark, obviously waiting for the command to attack the intruders.

"Ah!" the Marquis said, and his face was lit with a cold mischief that made Jermyn want to retch. "*Stand*, Greatheart—Master Eschar offers me no threat. In fact, I believe we understand each other quite well."

The dog settled back, clearly disturbed but obedient. Eschar bowed slightly in his chair. "I believe we do."

"Shall we say—ten thousand?"

"A round number," the Theoretician said judiciously. "But I also believe I mentioned that I do not deal in paltry sums."

The Lumianskan looked taken aback. "You rate your services highly."

"As do you and your prince. It is not only my silence which you are purchasing, Marquis, but my continued lack of curiosity—and you must know that that does not come cheap."

"Are you sure your word will be sufficient to quell this inquiry?"

"To redirect it, certainly," Eschar said, unmoved. "*If* I have the word to begin at once, and with sufficient motivation to act swiftly."

"I don't—" He hesitated. "You understand, I have no authority to authorize the dispersal of very large sums. It will take time to contact my superiors."

"You have little time," the Theoretician said. "Inspector Andrews is quite competent, and he will be back soon—with a search warrant."

"This Embassy has diplomatic immunity," Devereux said automatically. "He can't touch me here."

"He can with the Regent's permission," Eschar said coolly. "Which will not be long in arriving. Come, come, Marquis, let's not dawdle. I'm not asking for payment on account—merely some sign that we have an agreement."

The Marquis hesitated a long moment, then nodded. "Very well."

He crossed over to one of the bookcases and pressed on a section of carving. At once, the shelves swung free of the wall, revealing a concealed safe.

"You understand that I cannot give you anything in writing," he said. "And that it will take time to get the necessary funds from Lumiansk."

"I understand," Eschar said.

The Marquis turned to him again, in time to see the wolfhounds focusing on the screened end of the room again. The female growled, a deep, ominous sound, but Devereux was too caught up in what he was doing to pay attention. He had a savage smile on his face, and his fist was clenched around a silvery object.

"What I can offer you—is this!"

Meggan cried out, and Jermyn almost choked over a warning.

"Master Eschar," he said frantically, straightening up so suddenly that he toppled the screen and Delia almost fell off his shoulder. "Don't look! It's the Persuasion coin!"

"Only one of them, Jermyn," Eschar said, holding up an identical silver disk in his hand. "Careless of you to forget this one, Devereux. You might have known my apprentice would bring it to me."

The Marquis hissed, his face a lipless mask of rage. The other white gold coin glowed against his palm. "Where did you get that? I lost—"

"So you thought you'd lost it," Eschar said, amused. "You really should have known better. No bespelled object is ever truly lost. It resonates to its point of origin—so!"

197

He held Jermyn's coin out in front of him, so that his hand and the Marquis's were almost touching.

"Shall we see what happens when you hold both?"

"No!" The Lumianskan was breathing heavily, unable to move away. "You have no right—"

"You bring a plague down on this city and you say I have no right?" Eschar hurled at him.

"I didn't!" the Marquis insisted. "Goddess, do you think I wanted the weather wizards sick? I need them."

"What for?"

"To—to control the weather."

"Why?"

The Marquis hesitated, and Eschar held the coins closer, so that the glow from each overlapped at the edges. A faint, irritating hum filled the air. "What did you want the weather to do?"

"For Goddess's sake, keep them apart," the Marquis almost shrieked. "We wanted to damage the harvests. Not enough to cause famine, but enough to make people dissatisfied. Hungry people are ripe for rebellion, and we thought—"

"You thought to disrupt the Empire and perhaps win a little power for yourself in the process," Eschar said grimly. "Was your prince in on this pleasant little plot?"

"No."

Eschar took another step forward and the Marquis

cowered visibly. "Prince Reynald knows nothing of this. He's old and sick."

"Possibly," Eschar said, stepping back and putting the coin into his pocket. "Though we'll see what the Regent has to say. Do not be so foolish or self-sacrificing as to claim that you were in on this alone, Devereux. Now that we have the spell placed on the coins, we should be able to use them to trace your accomplices easily enough."

"What you know is of no consequence," the Marquis said, released from the paralysis caused by the overlapping spells. White and trembling, he looked from the young people at the end of the room to the Theoretician as if he couldn't believe the evidence of his eyes. "What these *children* may say is of even less consequence. Tracer! Greatheart! Take them!"

He dropped the wolfhounds' leads and dashed for the door. One beast sprang for Master Eschar's throat while the other hurled itself at the end of the room. Jermyn cried out incoherently, tumbling Delia off his shoulder and leaping in front of Meg. Landing on the floor, Delia looked up at the dogs, grunted loudly, and stamped her feet. The wolfhound heading toward her skidded to a stop, turned tail, and fled howling after its master. Its mate yelped once in surprise, performed a surprisingly acrobatic twist in midair, and followed.

"Dee, don't," Jermyn cried, grabbing for her. She

chittered at him and squirmed in his grasp, but he held firm. "You can't spray in here—this is a *library!*"

Master Eschar stood up and began straightening his clothing. "Don't scold, Jermyn. Her intervention was both timely and appropriate. I own, I hadn't considered that he might bring those brutes in with him. Meggie, are you all right?"

"Yes, sir," she said. Her face was pale and her eyes wide. Jermyn took her hand and was not surprised to find it cold and trembling.

"Rest easy, child," her guardian said, concerned and soothing. "Both of you, relax. We'll soon be away from here—"

"The Marquis!" Jermyn cried, remembering. "He'll get away!"

"He will not," Eschar said cheerfully. He held the silver coin out so they could see that it was glowing again. "He's still carrying the match to this coin, and the spell is still activated. Pity no one thought to warn him about what happens when the same man fixes the same spell onto identical objects, and those identical objects are brought into proximity. The spell has already begun to affect him as he would have used it to affect others—it should hit full strength before he gets half a block beyond any door in this building, around which the Inspector has stationed three full squads of men. The minute our friend the Marquis steps off Embassy grounds, he will forfeit his diplomatic immunity, his own Persuasion will make him temporarily amenable to any and every suggestion offered to him, and the constables will easily gather him in."

"You planned this all," Meggan said, outraged enough to forget her nervous reaction. She pulled away from Jermyn and stood up very straight. "You were using his own magic against him. And we were worried about you."

"Of course I planned it all. There was no need for you to worry. And let it be a lesson to you both, especially you, Jermyn," he said severely.

"A lesson in not worrying about my master?" he said, grinning with relief that everything was going to be all right.

"No. A lesson in your craft," the Theoretician told him. "As an apprentice, you must learn that only a fool relies on magic which he does not understand."

15

CONVULSIONS

Hours later, the rush of pleasure Jermyn had felt in the Lumianskan Embassy seemed like the most distant of dreams. He sat in Master Eschar's study with a splitting headache and the gloomy conviction that they were, if anything, further from a solution to the disease than they had been the day before.

Unlikely as it seemed, the Marquis had told the truth. He was not the one responsible for the plague.

"The evidence is quite clear," Eschar said finally, as if he wished it weren't. "We've run every test we can on the marked coins, and they have no connection whatsoever with this illness."

Inspector Andrews looked as if he were about to explode. "What do you mean, the coin can't be carrying the plague matrix? It's got to be!"

"It isn't," the Theoretician said.

Jermyn kept his eyes on the teacups he was refilling, trying not to let his hands shake as he did so. He didn't know why he bothered; no one really wanted tea. He'd just brought the tray in because Meggan had insisted.

Andrews wasn't giving up. "What tests did you run? Who was the wizard? With so many masters sick and unconscious—"

"We ran the Amstellaer Similarity Test," Eschar told him wearily. "On a scale of one to ten, the Marquis came out negative two, and you know what that means. We got a plus one on the coin itself, on the Sorcerous Revelations Scale, but no echo of Devereux, and that small a reaction is allowable within the margin of error. If he is involved in the plague, he has hidden the spell matrix far more thoroughly than I believed he would be able to hide it. Peter Quail, our wizard, is only a journeyman, it's true, but—"

"Well, there you are, then. He obviously made a mistake. We'll have to run the tests again."

"—*but*," Eschar repeated loudly, "he has sufficient power and understanding to enact both spells. And I

203

oversaw the procedures myself. They were accurate, I assure you. In addition, Jermyn was the first to handle the coin and I was next. Neither of us has contracted the plague—why not, if it is carrying the matrix? In my urgency to solve this puzzle, I foolishly overlooked the simple logic of that. I will not do so again."

"Well, what about the sign on that file of yours? The one your apprentice and young Meggan found?" Andrews was still fighting. "What does the noble Marquis say about *that?*"

"Not a great deal, because I haven't been able to confront him with it yet. You forget, he's in *your* custody now," Eschar said. "I've sent it to the Guild, to have more tests made as soon as Journeyman Quail recovers from the last round. Then we shall see."

"Are you sure it's safe to leave something like that lying around the Guild Hall? The Marquis might have agents to trigger the spell—"

"The Guild is the proper place to store any magical artifact," Eschar snapped. "I impressed upon my colleagues the need for security and careful handling of the file. If you do not trust us, then I suggest you take possession of the thing yourself."

Andrews appeared to collect himself. "I'm sorry, Theoretician. I didn't mean . . . but the Guild is disorganized, with so many masters sick and incapacitated. Devereux will have recovered from the

Persuasion overload by now. He could spring a trap of some sort, even from a holding cell."

"It doesn't take a master wizard to lock a box file in the vault and leave it alone," Eschar said sardonically. He was as tired as any of them, Jermyn realized—maybe more. "Especially not when I'm there to see it's done properly."

The Inspector went on doggedly: "Yes, I know, or I should have known. And I said I was sorry. But don't try to tell me that that slimy Lumianskan sewer rat wasn't up to something."

"I wouldn't dream of it," the Theoretician said wryly. "Of course he was. He was trying to disrupt the Empire by controlling its weather patterns. A nice plan, and one he and his backers had already begun to implement on the Continent. The man who controls weather patterns also controls the grain crop. The Marquis could have made a pretty sum speculating in agriculture, perhaps even enough to finance a revolution in Lumiansk."

"I don't understand," Jermyn said, looking up from the tea tray. "How could he already control the weather patterns on the Continent? I thought Lumiansk didn't have real wizards."

Eschar shrugged. "Some Guild wizards live overseas, and the Guild has trained the occasional Continental over the years. And as I've had occasion to tell you, where there are human beings, there will be workers of magic. We know so little about Continental magic that I can't really even theorize more completely."

"Is it possible that this plague is Continental magic?" Andrews said, looking suddenly hopeful. "If it is, maybe our tests wouldn't—"

"Tchah, Andrews, you know better than that. The Amstellaer tests the presence of magic, period, and the Revelations Scale is itself Continental in origin. No, the Marquis isn't even a particularly talented conspirator. We'd have caught on to his little scheme sooner rather than later. Spellcaster Douglas had already asked me to make a comparison of recent weather patterns for him."

"That proves my point," Andrews argued. "If the Lumianskan plot was so scatterbrained, what's more likely than for them to have a few other plans for disrupting the Empire? He'd already been paying off weather wizards, even the Weather Master. How long before he tried seducing earth wizards?"

"I almost wish he had tried," Eschar said, sitting up briskly. "Come, come, Inspector—if weather wizards are powerful and unpredictable, then earth wizards are literally beyond control! In any case, the Marquis tends to think in terms of political power, and earth wizards have very little of that."

"They are healers," Andrews said. "They're tied

to the earthmagic, and they can be active in the Guild and on the Council."

"They can be, but they rarely are," Eschar said. "Anyway, they'd be the first to notice something strange in an offer of white gold. You can't deceive a healer for long. That art sees too clearly into the hearts of others. And so far as I know, the only remaining true earth wizard of master rank is Jean Allons, who is far too old to be interested in foreign employment."

"The Spellmaker? Still alive?" the Inspector said, diverted. "I thought she died years ago."

"She's alive but living retired in the North, and is no longer available even for emergencies," Eschar said impatiently. "Don't change the subject, Andrew. The fact of the matter is, and remains, that we still have a plague matrix to find."

"Yes, yes, I know you're right," the Inspector said. "I just didn't want to admit it, even to myself. I still can't believe the coin isn't involved—it is the only common denominator we've found."

"Not completely," Eschar said. "There is Master Douglas, though I won't believe that *he* was on Lumianskan retainer."

"Of course not, but he's old, more susceptible to contagion—you said as much yourself. And hadn't he worked with Fulke, at least?"

Eschar frowned. "As Spellcaster, Steen Douglas works with every master wizard in the city, sooner or later. He even visits this house frequently, just to discuss theory with me."

"Yes, but he wouldn't have worked any magic—practical magic with you," Andrews said. "In any case, what difference does it make? If he didn't catch the plague from Fulke, he must have gotten it from someone Fulke gave it to. It's the *original* plague vector we care about, and that's the Weather Master. He was the first to fall ill, that night. That's what matters."

"True," Eschar said slowly. He looked suddenly abstracted. "And yet I wonder if that is *all* that matters. Andrew, have you a list of those who have been affected by the plague and those who had taken Devereux's offers?"

"Yes, of course, but not with me. Why? You've seen both lists."

"I'd like to see them again, if you please. Together, this time."

Andrews looked at him narrowly. "You've thought of something."

"Possibly. But you know me better than that. I refuse to act on supposition, especially after that debacle at the embassy."

The Inspector stood up. "Well, then I'd better get you what you want. Come to think of it, I should have at least the list of the sick in my carriage. The other is on my desk at the Constabulary, but I can get it later."

When he'd left, Jermyn silently started collecting the unused tea things. Master Eschar didn't seem to notice him; he was examining the single Lumianskan coin he'd retained for study.

"Sir?" Jermyn asked. "What's a spellmaker?"

"Eh?" Eschar looked up. "Oh, that. What *did* your aunt teach you? No wonder—never mind. I don't suppose it's relevant to daily wizardry, at that. A spellmaker is the practical equivalent of my own kind of magician."

"A—a practicing theoretician?"

"Not exactly." He shoved the coin into the top of his desk and firmly shut the drawer. "A spellmaker manipulates the earthmagic, creating new spells for all wizards to use. Hence the name."

"And Mistress Allons is one?" Jermyn asked, fascinated. "Are spellmakers very powerful?"

"Lady Jean—she's earned the title, with her service to the Crown. Yes, she is very powerful. She was my apprentice-master, before you ask how I know. And also before you ask, spellmakers are barred by law from sitting on Council."

"Why?"

Eschar chuckled tiredly. "A spellmaker can no more refrain from making spells than she can from breathing, and political magics are among the last needs of this or any land! Besides, there is no reason to appoint a Master Spellmaker. There seldom seems to be more than one full earth wizard—one master—in any given generation, except for healers. Perhaps because the need for healing is so much greater than the need for other kinds of magic."

"Master Eschar . . ." Inspector Andrews stood in the doorway, his face drawn with defeat. "William, I'm so sorry."

"What is it?" Eschar said, his voice suddenly harsh. Jermyn felt cold with fear: but if it were Merovice, surely Mrs. Dundee would have come herself?

"One of my men just brought word," Andrews said compassionately. "Master Douglas has just died. I thought you'd like to know before they rang him out. I know he was a friend of yours . . ."

Eschar looked down. His hands trembled slightly. "He was my father's friend before he was mine," he said, almost inaudibly. "Every theoretician needs a Guild sponsor, since we have no practical talent, and Steen Douglas believed in my potential enough to perform that service for me. He introduced me to Lady Jean, and she accepted me as her apprentice. In all my years, I never knew a finer wizard—or a better man."

Outside, distantly, bells began to ring in the three-five-seven pattern of prime numbers that signified the death of a master wizard, followed by the deep note of the solitary Temple bell tolling up the years of a man's life. Steen Douglas's life, though long, had nonetheless ended before its natural time. Jermyn felt very close to tears. It could so easily have been Aunt Merry. *It could still be.*

The Theoretician took a deep breath. "His will not be the last death if we do not do something."

"That's true enough," Andrews said, sounding discouraged. "Here's the list of the sick—it was in my carriage. Have you any new suggestions for me?"

"No," Eschar said. "Go home, Inspector, or go back to the Constabulary if you must, but get some rest. When you wake, bring me that second list and we'll go back to the beginning and start over. There must be something we've missed."

"Very well." Andrews turned to go, but paused in the door. "I'll leave a constable stationed at the front door in case you need to send for me."

"If I need you, I will come to you. Now go home!"

When he'd gone, the Theoretician turned to Jermyn. "That goes for you, too, young man. You're several hours behind on sleep, according to my calculations. Bed for you, and now."

"I was going to sit with Aunt Merry," Jermyn protested. "It's early yet."

"That's an order, Jermyn," Eschar said sternly. "Check in with Mrs. Dundee if you wish, and then go to bed. At least for a nap."

"You should rest too, sir," Jermyn said, worriedly noting lines in his master's face that hadn't been there the day before.

"I will, soon. I promise. Off with you, now."

Jermyn carried the tea tray back to the kitchen first. Meggan wasn't there. She must be tending to the linens, or the pantry. And Mrs. Dundee wouldn't let him see Aunt Merry; she shooed him off to bed as firmly as Master Eschar had.

"Your aunt's resting as well as can be," she said. "And you'll do her no good by staring at her with your eyes burned into black holes in your head."

Only Delia, sleepily curled up on the extra bed pillow in his temporary quarters, seemed glad to see him. She raised her head when he sat down next to her.

Je'm'n sleepy?

"No," he told her shortly. "But it seems I have to sleep anyway."

He lay down on the bed, fully clothed. His brain was buzzing with the events of the day, and he felt as if he couldn't hold still. After a few moments of restless squirming—which made Delia sit up and look at him anxiously—he resolutely closed his eyes and began to count sheep. But the sheep turned into black sheep, and then developed white striped fleeces and pointed, inquisitive noses. Soon he found himself counting skunks—who flatly refused to jump over gates or behave in any respectable, countable manner.

Delia chuckled at the back of his mind. *Silly.*

Very silly, he agreed with her crossly. *I can't sleep, and you aren't helping.*

Can't sleep, go eat, Delia said, logically.

I'm not hungry, he said, turning over.

Go for walk?

"No!"

That hurt her feelings so much that she curled up in a sulk. Jermyn sighed, but couldn't get up enough energy to apologize. He went back to trying to sleep.

He had finally achieved a light, restless doze when something made him open his eyes again. Not a sound, exactly, but—someone calling his name?

"Delia? I'm sorry, Dee. Are you that upset? I didn't mean—" A gentle snore answered him. He leaned over and stroked her awake. *Deedee?*

Her bright eyes blinked at him. *Go sleep, Je'm'n.*

"I can't. I—" He swung his feet to the side of the bed and sat up. "Something's wrong."

Agreeably, she padded over to sit beside him. *Hmm?*

"I don't know what," he said, more puzzled than worried. "It's just—"

Ahhhhhhhhhhhhhhhhhhhhhhhhhhhhhhhhhh—

The scream rang in his soul. Jermyn froze, the awful sound of it clanging through him, as sure as sanity would let him be that no one in the room had actually made a noise. Next to him, Delia whimpered. Without thinking, he caught her in his arms and headed for the door.

"Aunt Merry!" Her voice—no, it was Pol, crying out that his mistress was in desperate trouble. The blood connection between aunt and nephew sent him hurtling down the hall almost before he had time to think where he was going.

He flung open the door to Merovice's bedroom to see Mrs. Dundee trying frantically to straighten his aunt's twisting, convulsing body. Behind her, Meggan hovered anxiously. Jermyn barely had time to think— *but Meggan isn't allowed in the sickroom!*—before he felt his aunt's pain, agony slicing into him like a hot knife through butter. Pol, awake and bolt upright, fur on end, hissed in incoherent fury and rage at the bedside.

"The water, Meggie, full in her face," Mrs. Dundee was saying. "That's it. We've got to shock her out of it."

"Jermyn!" Meggan said. "You shouldn't be here. Your aunt—"

"She's gone into convulsions," Mrs. Dundee said, not looking up. "It's happened with others, I'm told. We've got to calm her down."

"Pol's awake. Can he help?"

"He could if we could reach him," she panted. "He's shocked awake, no more aware than she is, and we can't hold her. Don't let her twist her back like that. She'll hurt herself."

Jermyn struggled to control his aunt's writhing body. This was worse, infinitely worse, than Aunt Merry in a coma. She was in pain. He ignored Meggan's hand tugging insistently at his sleeve. There had to be something he could do. *There has to be!*

Delia's mind touched his, filling him with the warm strength of the familiar-bond. Taking a deep breath, he reached out along the bond, using the connection to the little skunk to access the power within himself. He could reach Delia: Delia could reach Pol—and the link that went from familiar to wizard would still be in place, even with Fulke's curse blocking it from wizard to familiar. If he could reach Aunt Merry through her familiar, *force* calming into her . . .

He ignored Mrs. Dundee's desperate efforts, and concentrated. There, there were the nodes of power— the lines leading out of himself. There was the blood link to Merovice, and there was Aunt Merry herself, pulsing white with pain and terror. There were Delia and Pol. All he had to do was touch the pain.

"No, Jermyn!" Meggan's voice, filled with fear, came from someplace outside and far away. "If you touch her mind, you'll catch it too!"

Absently, he closed off his ears. Nothing mattered but Merovice. She needed him—even Pol needed him—and Delia was a steady, strong presence holding him firm. He reached, balanced—let a bit of power flow this way, flow that way—and he was inside.

Pain! Ah, Powers, it hurts so much worse from within. He was at the center of a maelstrom of brilliantly hued memories, jagged images from his aunt's mind. They filled the nightmare in which she was trapped, and which he now shared with her. The bright colors swirling around him made him dizzy. Tentatively at first, then with increasing assurance, he began to slow them down. *Is this like what healers do, when they heal?* He could sense his own heart, beating in ragged time with Merovice's, and he made a conscious effort to slow both beats. Gradually his breathing became regular, even; hers followed suit. Her body stilled, and the raging fever that had caused the convulsions eased slightly. *Quiet, calm. Be still.*

When at last he opened his eyes, he was sitting on the edge of the bed. Aunt Merry, *praise be to the Powers*, was lying still again, breathing in a steady rhythm, and Pol was stretched out limply beside her.

Meggan was staring at him white-faced, and Mrs. Dundee looked perturbed.

Delia nuzzled his chin, and he managed a weak smile. "It's all right, everybody. How's Aunt Merry?"

"As she was," Mrs. Dundee said. "Lad, that was a dangerous thing you did. Have you any training in the healing arts?"

"No." He tried to stand; the world spun and he almost fell. Meggan reached to support him.

"Keep your distance," Mrs. Dundee said.

"But—" She looked even more frightened. "He can't have it so soon."

"Be that as it may, now he's been contaminated

for certain." She looked at Jermyn. "Are you strong enough to reach your room?"

"Yes, of course." He braced himself, and tried standing again. This time, he made it. "I'm fine. For now. I'd better go tell Master Eschar what's happened."

"I'll go with you," Meggan said, but Mrs. Dundee stopped her.

"You'll stay with me," she said firmly. "Bad enough you came in here. I'm not having you any more involved. Don't fret, lass. If anyone can solve this, it will be the Master."

"He will, Meg. You know that," Jermyn said comfortingly. At least now he could stop waiting to get sick; it had come, and he would have to cope with it. "Just help Mrs. Dundee take care of Aunt Merry. Please? I can manage by myself. I promise."

Delia followed him down the stairs, thumping along on his heels as if she hadn't a care in the world. Strange, he'd have thought she'd be more affected by what had happened. Well, wait and see what Master Eschar had to say. It wasn't as late as he'd thought— not long past full dark. The Theoretician must still be in his study, puzzling over some idea or other. Jermyn wondered why he hadn't responded to all the commotion. Surely he wasn't that insensitive to wizardry? Even Meggan had clearly felt *something*. Well, maybe he was thinking hard.

The study door was ajar, letting out a stream of

golden lamplight into the hallway. Jermyn pushed at the panel carelessly, swinging it the rest of the way open.

"Master?" he called. "Master, I'm sorry to disturb you, but—"

He stopped, almost as stunned with horror as he had been upstairs. The Theoretician was sitting slumped over his desk, his right hand stretched out before him, fingers curved under the palm. Jermyn didn't need to look at the white face or hear the steady, shallow breathing to know what was wrong.

"He isn't even a practicing wizard," he said stupidly. "Why should he go so suddenly, and not me?"

He reached out to take the Master's pulse, and found that the fingers of the right hand were more than just closed; they were clenched tightly around something. Delia pulled impatiently at his boot top, curious, but he ignored her. What had Eschar been holding that was so important? One by one he loosened the curled fingers, to reveal a familiar white gold disk.

The Lumianskan coin. Master Eschar had put it away in his desk, which meant that he must have taken it out again—perhaps even deliberately reached for it as he felt himself being stricken.

"But—he said the Marquis couldn't be involved in the plague," Jermyn said, turning the coin in his hands. "He believed it. Why should he—oh!"

He caught his lower lip between his teeth, and pressed his own fist so tightly around the coin that the metal bit into his palm.

"So that's what it is," he whispered, sadly. "What it meant."

He sank down into the leather chair and put his head in his hands.

16

REVELATIONS

MRS. DUNDEE was understandably upset when she heard the news. Jermyn and the constable from the front door carried Master Eschar up to his room while she fluttered about trying to make him comfortable.

"Oh, the poor man," she said, distracted. "He's never ill. I don't know what we shall do."

"The best we can, Mrs. Dundee," Meggan said, though her eyes sought Jermyn's for reassurance. "Won't we?"

"We'll have to," he said heavily. "Mrs. Dundee, Meg, I'll have to inform the Guild what's happened.

And I'll get myself checked over at the same time," he said, forestalling their objections. "Though it doesn't look like I'm coming down with anything. I feel fine."

"You look well enough," Mrs. Dundee said doubtfully. "I must say."

"Yes, ma'am." He took a deep breath. "I think I'll stop at the Constabulary, too. I was going to send Inspector Andrews a message, but maybe I'd better go myself and then Constable—um—"

"Thumm, sir," the man said, touching his forehead. "Constable Thumm."

"Thank you—then Constable Thumm can stay here in case you need any help."

"We'll be all right," Meggan said stoutly.

She walked him down to the front door, and stood watching him put on his cloak. "Better tie the hood up. It's raining outside."

"It's dark, too. Do we have a lantern?"

"You can borrow my hand lamp," Thumm volunteered. "I can make do with the spare."

"Thank you again." He looked up and saw Mrs. Dundee on the stairs. She looked worried, and he nodded at her as reassuringly as he could. "Meg, Mrs. Dundee needs you now. Look after Delia for me, will you? I've told her to stay in the study. And don't worry if I'm a bit long getting back. I want to ask about that box file we looked at this morning. Master

Eschar left it at the Guild, and Inspector Andrews was fretting about it being safe there."

"Jermyn," Meggan said, her eyes round, "do you think that file had anything to do with Master Eschar's getting sick?"

"I don't know," he said grimly, "but I intend to find out."

"What file?" the housekeeper asked from the stairs.

"Meg will tell you," he said, and hesitated. "Be good, now."

Taking hold of his courage, he leaned forward to kiss Meggan's forehead lightly. Her eyes filled with tears, but she didn't flinch or pull away.

"Be careful, Jermyn," she whispered.

"I will," he told her, not meeting her eyes. She was so beautiful—so vulnerable, it almost broke his heart. "Don't worry. I'll be as quick as I can."

The streets outside were dark and empty. Most of the streetlights were mere flickers, with no one to renew the master spells. Any more of this, and the city would start to look like it had hundreds of years ago, when the land was newly settled. Jermyn kept Constable Thumm's hand lamp directed at his feet, so that he could watch his footing. He knew the way to the Guild Hall well enough.

The clerk at the front desk was suitably grieved to hear about Master Eschar. He said he would inform the Council, or whoever was acting as the Council these days. Jermyn left him to it.

The other part of his errand was more difficult, but when he finally set out in search of Inspector Andrews, he had the green box file under his arm. The wind was raw with approaching winter; he shivered inside his cloak, and missed Delia's warm weight on his shoulder. But it was a natural cold, with none of the heavy feeling the weather had had lately. The climate was recovering, becoming normal again, even without a Weather Master to help. Poor Fulke—had he even had the slightest idea of what he was getting into when he'd started this mess?

"No, no more deaths," Inspector Andrews said, yawning. Despite his obvious exhaustion, he looked serious: Master Eschar's illness had shaken him as much as it had Jermyn. "The worst so far is that Healer—Collins? And the Weather Master."

"Aunt Merry's bad too," Jermyn told him, as calmly as he could. He wiped sweaty palms on the inside of his cloak. "But Master Eschar seems to be holding his own. Of course, it's only the early days yet, for him."

"Oh, you can't kill that man," Andrews said, as if he were trying to convince himself. "He's indestructible."

"Yes. Aunt Merovice is, too, usually." Jermyn looked at the file he'd set on Andrews's desk. "I've been wondering about that, and about other things, too. Listen—"

When he'd finished, the Inspector was white and drawn with dismay.

"I don't understand," he said heavily. "*Why?*"

"That I don't know," Jermyn admitted. "I've got some suspicions, but no way to prove them. Only—well, can you see anything else it could be?"

"No," Andrews said. He was silent. "The question is, what do we do about it?"

"We have to act fast," Jermyn said. "Too many people will die, if we don't."

Andrews's eyes narrowed. "You have an idea," he said.

"I think so. I've been to the Guild, and they say that Journeyman Quail is recovered enough to run some more tests."

"On the box file? Then why did you bring it here to me?"

"Because I don't want him to run the tests in the Guild Hall. I think that would be—would be more or less what someone wanted all along. Don't you?"

"Powers, yes." The Inspector looked even more shaken. "I hadn't thought—can we perform them here? Our lab is rudimentary, compared to Guild facilities, but we could—"

"No. Not here either. It would work, in the end, but it would take too long. Instead, why don't we—"

He talked for a quarter hour. When he finished, the Inspector was dubious.

"I don't like it," he said. "It's too risky—you'd be alone. Couldn't we wait and bring in someone from outside the quarantine area to back you up?"

"That would take too long, too," Jermyn said. He ran his fingers through his hair. "Besides, I'm the only one who has a chance of making this look natural— if we hurry. It has to be done while I'm still able. I might—I might turn white and fall over any moment myself. I don't really know why I haven't, yet."

Andrews nodded, still worried but convinced. "I suppose it's worth a try. I just wish we had a healthy master wizard left in the city."

"Don't underestimate any journeyman," Jermyn said, smiling slightly. "Even Peter Quail."

The house on Wisteria Street was quiet and dark when he let himself in the front door; it would be dawn soon. Delia poked her nose out from behind the umbrella stand.

Je'm'n?

All serene, sweetheart, he said in a soft mind-voice. *All set. Have you been keeping watch?*

Uh-huh. Waiting. She formed pictures: Mrs. Dundee was upstairs in Master Eschar's room; Aunt Merry and Pol slept in false peace, under Meggan's watchful eye.

Let's get on with it, then, he said, picking her up and setting her on his shoulder.

The study seemed worse than empty without Master Eschar in it. The fire had died down, and the gaslights burned low. Jermyn waved two of them out and raised the third, the one over the desk, to a soft glow. He wouldn't need much light. Seating himself at the great desk with a small shiver—this was Master Eschar's place—he pulled out the box file, the file he'd fetched for Master Douglas, which had found its way into Fulke's hands. Inspector Andrews had reluctantly let him take it home.

He opened it: wavy lines, graphs, some columns of arcane figures in Eschar's small, precise handwriting. Carefully, he squinted against the dim light, instinctively reaching out through his link to Delia, who was clinging to her special pad on his shoulder. This was the part that Inspector Andrews hadn't liked: he was going to have to activate the matrix again, taking his chances with getting sick right now. But he had to do it. He had to attract the attention of the plague spell's guardian.

There—what was that, outlined in the scattered mist? Dim, shadowy letters taking shape began to glow softly, as if on fire. An ornate *M* intertwined with an *L*, like on the Marquis's coin, yet—unlike. These letters had fewer curlicues, were straighter, more regular and easier to read. Why hadn't he noticed the difference before? *Because you weren't looking for it*, he acknowledged soberly. *Devereux was enough of a villain for you, and you never looked beyond him and Fulke as his servant. You never looked at things the other way around.*

"So now you know," said a voice from the door.

"I know," he said sadly. "We were so convinced it was a title, we never thought of proper names. *M* and *L*—Meggan O'Loughlin. Meggan *of* Loughlin."

Dark eyes fathoms deep in the lamplight, she looked straight at him expressionlessly. "Not Meggan. Malory."

"What do you mean?" he asked.

"I'm not Meggan. I'm Malory O'Loughlin," she told him, tossing her head. "Meggan is the one people hurt."

"I see," he said slowly. "Is Malory the one with the magic-working ability?"

"Of course," she said, smoothing her hair self-consciously. "What would clumsy Meg do with power? She'd be afraid to use it. Father knew better than to give the spell to *her*."

227

"Your father is the one who created the plague matrix, then?"

"He did." She paused, frowning. "He was a wizard, a real wizard, but people couldn't know. They were evil—nasty. We had to trick them. We did, too, didn't we? I tricked *you* all by myself. Little Meggan didn't help a bit. How did you find out?"

"Once I knew who had set the trap, it wasn't difficult to figure," he told her honestly. "The original contagion vectors—the wizards who were carriers— were all people who had visited this house. Master Douglas, Aunt Merry. We all thought Fulke carried the disease to Aunt Merry, through the curse, but it was the other way around. She infected him, and through him every weather wizard in the city. And Spellcaster Douglas was often here. He gave the plague to Healer Collins, his personal healer, and then she gave it to everyone she tried to help—and to everyone in the fire circle. That was a bit of luck for you, the fire."

She sniffed. "Luck had nothing to do with it. I *planned*. Sooner or later, I knew there'd be an emergency, and who more likely to be at the center of it than the head of the Council of Wizards?"

"It must have been partly luck," he insisted. "What was this file, a trap that didn't work?"

She scowled at him indecisively, and began to chew a strand of long blond hair. "The Spellcaster was going to take that box with him to Council," Meggan said. "If he had, the whole Council would have gotten sick—it was triggered to spring when it was opened. You saw that, but then I was with you when it happened and I had to hold it off. I don't think that fool Fulke ever opened it. If he had, it would have been almost as good, but he just *didn't*. Weather wizards!"

He couldn't help smiling. "Aunt Merovice would agree with you. The only thing I don't understand is—why, Meggan? What did the Empire ever do to you?"

"Not the Empire!" she said, flaring. Her eyes blazed, and her features went taut with emotion. "The Empire never did anything—it was the wizards. Foul magicians, all of them, the black art in another form. A *Guild*, they call it, but that isn't right—guilds are for decent people, craftsmen. Not wizards. They made my father love that witch, my mother. She enchanted him. He was a priest. He knew magic was evil, but he couldn't help but love her. He had the art, she said, and he should learn to use it. She said she'd teach him, and then it killed her and finally him, and almost me, until for a while there was only Meggan left. And oh, it hurt so bad I couldn't stand it. I didn't even want to come out of the dark. Papa, I'm afraid of the dark—"

He nodded. "That's why your talent didn't show

when you came to live with Master Eschar. You were Meggan then, not Malory, and Malory is the wizard."

"I'm not!" she shrilled. "I—I just have the power. Father gave it to me. He said—he said when I was afraid, I would make others afraid, and that would be his revenge. When a person gets scared enough, he can't stand it: he just goes away into the darkness in his own mind and stays there. Father knew that. He knew if he could drive the wizards into the darkness, he could end this—this contagion of magic. But he had to test it—he had to—and Mama was dead, so he, so he—"

"So he tested it on you," Jermyn said softly, filled with a terrible pity. Meggan was the true devil's child, the daughter of a madman who used and abused her to further his insane scheme. "And the trigger emotion is fear. In order to test it, he had to make you afraid—not just once, but again and again. Was that it? Then, when he was sure, he set the spell matrix into your power, so that any attempt to touch your basic talent would activate it. And that final nightmare drove you—drove you inside yourself for a long time. When you came out—when Master Eschar brought you here—you found that Meggan was in control of things. And the only way you could act was to do what your father had wanted you to do. To use the plague matrix."

She went very still. "Well. Now you know."

"Yes." He sighed. "Why did you wait so long to get Master Eschar?"

Her eyes flickered uncertainly, but she managed a disdainful sneer. "He only *studied* magic. There's nothing wrong with that, or not much. But then he was getting close to finding out, I could tell, so I had to stop him."

He looked at her compassionately. Funny, he had expected to hate the one who'd brought the plague to the city, who'd hurt Aunt Merry—as he'd hated Fulke for cursing her. But he couldn't bring himself to hate Meggan.

"Meg, we can help you," he said slowly. "Master Eschar knew there was something wrong. That's why he was so understanding, and why he hadn't sent you to school yet."

"I don't want your help," she cried, her hands working like claws. "I'm Malory, not Meggan. *Malory!* And Malory doesn't need *anyone's* help."

"You're going to get help whether you want it or not," he said. "When I tell Inspector Andrews what I found tonight—"

"Who says he's going to hear of it?" she asked, hair falling into her eyes. "You should never have brought the file home, Jermyn. You should have left it at the Guild, for others to get sick from it. The spell is activated now, and I'm not going to hold it back this time."

"Inspector Andrews is coming tomorrow morning," Jermyn said calmly, though his heart was beating fast. If only he could have Meggan back again. Meggan was fond of him, was fond of Master Eschar. "*This* morning, really. It's just a few hours away. He's going to bring a journeyman so we can run some tests here, to see if it was the file that infected Master Eschar. Now we won't need any more tests. I'll tell Inspector Andrews, and he'll take you to the Guild, and that will be that. You didn't attack quite enough wizards, Meg. Or Malory, or whoever. The Guild may be down, but it's not out yet, and it won't be hard to connect you to the plague. Blood tells, after all—your father built the spell matrix, and you triggered it. The link will be clear."

Malory wasn't fond of anyone. Her smile widened ferally, and she lifted her left hand to point. "Only if you are around to tell him about it."

The letters had faded from the air over the file; now they sprang back into vivid life, and the papers within burst into flames. With a cry, Jermyn leaped to his feet. He grabbed the fireplace sand bucket and heaved its contents over the desk—too late! The fire went out, but the box file, paper, initials, and all, were charred scraps of nothingness and ash.

"There!" Malory said triumphantly. "I knew I would have to give it to you sooner or later, even if you didn't get it through your aunt. Can you feel it, Jermyn? I've fixed it right on you, from me to you, and there's no way to avoid that. Even Master Eschar couldn't. That rush of fear you just felt—that means the plague is activating. By the time Inspector Andrews gets here, you'll be unconscious—just like all the others."

Jermyn swayed slightly, but remained standing. Delia settled herself against his neck. "Thank you, Meg."

"Malory," she said automatically, then stopped. "What do you mean—Thank you? I just gave you the plague. I've killed you, fool."

"Not yet," he told her, coming out from behind the desk. "And we should be able to cure everyone, now that we can deactivate the spell matrix. Inspector Andrews? Did you hear?"

The Inspector stepped out from behind the long curtains over the study windows. "I heard," he said grimly. "Journeyman Quail?"

Peter Quail was standing next to him, hands spread and glowing wand in one of them. "The scent of magic is unmistakable," he said importantly. "She's the plague wizard, all right."

Meggan whirled for the door. The Inspector moved over to block her way. In through the window poured constables, constables, and more constables into the room.

"It was her father," Jermyn said, trying to explain. "He built the spell, fixed it into her—into her talent.

Into her self. He must have been a pretty powerful wizard, but I don't think he was quite sane. Meggan's just as much a victim as anyone, Inspector."

"That's for the Guild to decide," Peter said, righteously. "She caused Master Douglas's death, disrupted the city, cost thousands in damages, and embarrassed the Guild. She'll have to pay for all that."

Meggan's face had gone the color of old bone. Her eyes flamed. She flung out both hands at once, and the shimmer of the plague matrix that was her initials appeared in the air between them. It held for a moment, and then she snarled. "Take them! Take them all!"

"Meg," Jermyn cried, too late. *How could I be so careless?* He had known she could activate the matrix directly. Peter Quail was no match for her: he whimpered once and sagged to the floor. Even Inspector Andrews gagged. "Meg, don't. Don't you see? It's *over*."

"Goddess take you," she hissed at him. "Goddess take you straight to the fire! Why don't you fall? You, most of all—she *liked* you. *I* liked—"

The magic rushing through the room kept the Inspector and his men frozen in place. Andrews's face writhed with the effort to move, to give commands, to hold back his fear. *Everyone has some psychic ability*, Master Eschar had said, and now he was seeing the truth of that statement. Only Jermyn seemed immune to the spell. When he felt Delia move uneasily on his shoulder, he suddenly knew why.

Agonizingly slowly, he took one step forward. It was like walking through deep water, through warm molasses, through quicksand. He steadied himself, reached mentally to Delia to tighten the link between them, and took another step.

"It won't work on me," he said, fighting for coherence. She backed away, stunned, until the wall stopped her. "You should know by now that I'm different."

"You can't be," she choked. "I never . . . before, I didn't want you sick. If it happened, it happened, but I wasn't going to *try* to hurt you."

"So you hurt Aunt Merry," he said grimly. "I suppose you thought that was all right?"

Her eyes were wide with shock. "Keep away from me!"

"You should have known," he told her, taking another step. Delia balanced herself on his shoulder, digging her claws into the pad that had been Meggan's idea, and crooned to him encouragingly. "You should have realized. Did you ever hear of a wizard with a skunk for a familiar before? Skunks are different—not like cats, or birds. Better in some ways, not in others—but different, always."

It was so simple, really, when he thought of it. *Cats are graceful, proud, selfish, and sleek. A skunk*

235

is awkward, short, peace-loving—and fearless. A skunk fears very little, because it has very little to fear. Even from mankind.

"The plague matrix is triggered by the victim's own fear," he told her. "Aunt Merry was afraid I wouldn't come back after I stormed out. Master Douglas was afraid the city would burn. Fear is what does it. But because of Delia, my fear is neutralized."

"You have to be afraid," she whispered, raising her arms to cover her face. For a moment it was Meggan looking at him out of terrified brown eyes. "Everyone is afraid of *something*. Everyone . . ."

"Oh, I'm afraid," he said. "As afraid as you are right now—maybe even more. But Delia blocks the spell."

He caught her wrists and pulled them behind her, breaking her connection to the plague matrix. In the center of the room, it glimmered softly, and slowly melted away. Meggan struggled against him for a moment, and then went limp, sobbing helplessly. Delia inched forward along the pad to sniff the wheat-gold hair.

Funny smell, she remarked, tilting an inquiring eye at her master. It was the same thing she'd repeated when he'd set her on Master Eschar's desk the night before. *Funny bad smell.*

"Yes," Jermyn said softly, reaching up to stroke Meggan's hair. Inspector Andrews came forward, his eyes warm with concern and relief. "Of course you wouldn't recognize *that* odor mixed with the magic, Dee. You've never smelled it near at hand. Only from a distance."

The scent of human fear.

17

ENDINGS AND BEGINNINGS

THE LATE AFTERNOON sun gilded the book-shelves and touched the unaccustomed finery decking the library: a snow-white tablecloth, the silver tea set, platters of scones and biscuits and baked meats and cream buns. Mrs. Dundee had really outdone herself, Jermyn thought in amusement, giving the tablecloth one last twitch.

Delia stood on her hind legs, sniffing.

"Don't you dare," he told her sternly. "This is people food. You'll get yours later."

Clearly she didn't feel like waiting. With a guilty look around the empty room, he slipped her one of the chocolate biscuits. After all, she'd earned a reward.

It was almost a week since Inspector Andrews and his men had taken Meggan away. With her in custody, the plague spell unraveled, and the plague itself had begun to respond to treatment. Meggan didn't have the knowledge to recast her father's spell herself, even if she'd been stable and aware enough to try—which she wasn't. Healer Collins had been among the first to recover, and she said that Meggan might be cured in time, but that it would *take* time. What her father had done to her, the abuse she'd lived through, Jermyn still didn't like to imagine. He shivered in the bright room, remembering her cold, staring eyes as she was bundled into the prison carriage. There had been no sanity in those eyes—almost no life.

Voices echoed in the hall: Aunt Merry and Master Eschar. Grinning, Jermyn went to pull the door open.

"I tell you I am perfectly capable of walking by myself," Aunt Merry snapped.

"And I tell you that you've been ill," Eschar snapped right back.

"So have you," she argued.

"I was unconscious for one night. You were in a coma for days. Ah, Jermyn—good. Get your aunt settled by the fire, will you? I want to answer the door."

"You'll do nothing of the sort, Master," Jermyn said firmly. "Both of you, come in and sit down."

"But the door—"

"I feel fine—"

Jermyn raised his voice, drowning them both out. "Mrs. Dundee is perfectly capable of tending to the door, and so am I. Now come in and *sit down*, or we'll call this whole thing off."

Pol hissed at his mistress. He had recovered fairly quickly from his long sleep, but he knew how weak she still was, and he could smell the food in the library. Merovice glared at him.

"Humpf!" she said. "Betrayed by my own cat. Oh, very well, very well. I'm coming. William!"

"This is my house," he said, no less exasperated. "You'd think—"

"You'd think a grown Theoretician would have sense enough to sit down before he falls down," she told him tartly, settling herself firmly on the sofa. "Pol, get over here, boy. I need some cuddling. Sit down, William. You make me dizzy, swaying like that."

"I am not swaying. I was just—"

Jermyn left them to it and went to help Mrs. Dundee, who was just letting Inspector Andrews in.

"I'm sorry if I'm late," he said. "Last minute business."

"Are you certain they won't be wanting me to

serve, Jermyn?" Mrs. Dundee asked worriedly. "Your aunt can pour out, but she really shouldn't hand the cups around."

"I'll do it for her," Jermyn assured the housekeeper. She'd hesitantly announced that she had no desire to sit in on this meeting, not wanting to talk about Meggan if she didn't have to.

"It's all set, by the way," Andrews said to Jermyn, handing Mrs. Dundee his hat. "He'll be here. At the last minute, he tried to claim he was still too weak to go out—that's what delayed me. But I offered him the services of a constabulary healer, and then I left an escort to make certain nothing goes wrong. I just hope your master knows what he's doing."

"He usually does," Jermyn said, wishing he could be certain this time. "Come on. We're all set up in the library."

By the fire, Merovice was already doing the honors.

"Tea for you, William," she said briskly. "With plenty of cream and sugar—now, don't argue. You need the nourishment. Pol, my pretty, keep your whiskers out of that cream pitcher or I'll snip them off. Jermyn, where's your creature got to?"

Delia poked her head out from under the couch, her eyes sparkling mischievously as she eyed the table.

"Oh, she's around," Jermyn said vaguely, slanting his familiar a warning look. She twitched her nose at him and disappeared back under the couch. "Sir, Inspector Andrews is here—"

"So I see," Eschar said irritably. "Glad you could make it, Inspector. Do you know Merovice Graves?"

"We've met," Merovice said hospitably. "I was an expert witness in that mass poisoning case of his a few years back, William. Don't you remember? It's good to see you, Inspector. You're looking well."

"And you, Mistress Graves," Andrews said gallantly, taking the cup she handed him.

"I don't know what we're all here for anyway," Merovice said, slicing into a plum cake and giving Jermyn the plates to hand around. "We all know what happened. That poor child Meggan went mad and nearly did for the lot of us."

"It's a little more complicated than that, I'm afraid," Eschar said, sighing. "Meggan O'Loughlin is the child of two of the most talented wizards I've ever known. Her mother was a student of mine, and before me she studied with Lady Jean. We thought for a while that she might prove to be a spellmaker, but we were wrong."

"What did she lack?" Merovice asked around a mouthful of biscuit. "Not talent, if what you say is true."

"No. Not talent." Eschar stared into his teacup for a moment. "She was a beautiful girl, Alys—much like Meggan, only not so fair. We couldn't convince her that the absence of political and, to an extent, personal ambition was a prerequisite for true spell-making. When she failed her journeyman's exam, she couldn't stand it. I don't think she'd ever failed anything before."

"So she married a Lumianskan churchman," Jermyn said hastily, trying to banish the sad look from his master's eyes. "And the Lumianskan religion preaches against magic, doesn't it?"

"Yes, it does—like most Continental churches, to some degree or other. Young Manning O'Loughlin was one of the Lumianskan delegation, the season Alys went to work at the Embassy. He was quite devout, but he also had a strong and deeply suppressed talent which activated shortly after he met Alys, probably stimulated by her talent and his attraction to her."

"Sad, that," Merovice commented. "The last thing he would have wanted was magic, I imagine."

"Indeed," Eschar agreed somberly. "We warned Alys that she was asking for trouble, but she wouldn't listen. She claimed that Manning had come to terms with her magic, that he'd accepted her talent if not his own, and that they would work things out. Evidently, that wasn't the case."

"It might have been if they'd had more time," Inspector Andrews put in. "We've been getting reports from Lumiansk. Alys O'Loughlin died giving birth to her second child, when Meggan was about four or five years old. Her husband managed to find a Guild-trained healer for his wife when it became obvious that she was having trouble, but then she and the baby died anyway. It must have seemed to him that he'd defied the teachings of his church for nothing."

"Yes, that's logical," Eschar said. "I assume that O'Loughlin himself created this fear plague?"

"No, he seems to have found it in some book—nothing I've ever heard of, but I'm promised a copy as soon as the mail ship can make it over the water," Andrews said.

"Good. I'd like to see that. We know too little about Continental magic, as it is. Perhaps if we knew more, we might have been able to fight back more effectively."

"Might have, could have—not likely," Merovice said. "O'Loughlin must have been an incredible talent."

"Or Meggan," Jermyn said. He flushed when everyone turned to look at him. "Well, he'd set the spell-matrix into her—right into her personality. She didn't even realize it was there half the time."

"A twin personality," Eschar said. "One, helpless, timid, and loving, with little or no talent for sorcery. The other—"

"—vengeful and angry, with all the sorcery in the world locked into a single spell," Merovice finished for him. "Poor child. Poor, abused child."

Inspector Andrews cleared his throat. "What did alert you to the girl, sir? In the end."

Eschar smiled ruefully. "Process of elimination, I'm afraid. If it wasn't the Marquis, then who? You'd given me the list of those infected, Andrew, and while I was waiting for the other one, I studied it. I started to think about patterns of contagion, and common denominators—something I should have been doing all along, of course. And then I finally realized just how many of those affected had some connection to my house."

"Yes, we all should have seen that," Andrews said ruefully. "Douglas, Mistress Graves—I don't know how we missed it."

"Simple," Eschar said. "We were looking the wrong way. I'm not saying I would have reached the right conclusion, even that night. But I was sitting at my desk, puzzling over it, and all of a sudden there was Meggan, asking if I wanted any dinner."

"You must have reached into the desk drawer to get the coin when you felt yourself becoming ill and realized what—no, *who*—was the cause," Jermyn said, reaching for a biscuit. *Keep it casual, now— there's been enough grief.* "When I found it, I knew it had to be a clue you were trying to leave for us. Then I looked at it, really looked at it for the first time since I'd gotten it, and realized that since you couldn't have been thinking of the Marquis when you reached for it—well, it could be that just the initials were what mattered. And they were the same as Meggan's . . ."

"And that was that," Andrews finished for him.

Eschar looked away. "I should have known sooner, should have done more. When I found that she had no talent for magic, I was surprised, considering her parents' abilities. But sometimes it happens that way. If I'd investigated more fully, perhaps—"

"Don't, William," Merovice said gently. "You mustn't blame yourself. It's the girl's father who did this to her—the guilt is his."

"Yes. I suppose I must believe that." He watched the firelight, his face very still.

"And you, Jerry," Merovice said, rounding on her nephew fiercely, "let this be a lesson to you. Leave the guilt to those who deserve it. You'll earn enough of your own to satisfy."

He knew what she meant—that he shouldn't blame himself for what had happened to her. Swallowing a little, he reached over and touched her hand. "I know, Aunt Merry. I love you."

"Ah, now, no need to be getting sentimental," she said, embarrassed.

He opened his mouth to say something more, but Mrs. Dundee forestalled him by speaking from the library door.

"Sir?" she said. "There's a gentleman here—"

"Of course. Show him in," the Theoretician said,

sitting up. "Now, Merry, remember that this is my house. Mind your manners."

"Why, what a thing to say," Merovice said. "Who are you expecting, Princess Alexandra or the Regent?"

"Neither—"

It was Fulke, of course. Jermyn held his breath, hoping that he and Inspector Andrews, between them, would be able to prevent actual bloodshed. The Weather Master had lost weight during his ordeal, and his normally ruddy complexion had taken on a sallow hue. He was dressed for once in a sober, respectable brown.

In Aunt Merry's lap Pol stiffened and yowled warningly. Merovice herself gaped, and took a deep, outraged breath.

"Who let that—that overrated whining toady in here? William—"

"Calm yourself, Merovice," Eschar warned. "Weather Master Fulke is here by my invitation, and for a reason. Fulke? I believe you have something to say, don't you? Let's begin with that."

The Weather Master's eyes narrowed. He looked as if he would rather be having a tooth pulled.

"I'm sorry," he mumbled into his beard.

Merovice sat up, sparkling. "What did you say?"

"I'm sorry!" he roared. Delia squeaked and dove under Jermyn's chair. Her black eyes peered out in delighted mischief.

"And?" the Theoretician prompted meaningfully.

247

Fulke flushed an ugly red. "And I'll take the curse off. Soon."

"Today," Eschar said sternly. "Before you leave this house."

"Well, so that's what he's here for," Merovice said, clapping her hands. "And about time, too."

"Aunt Merovice," Jermyn said warningly. He caught her eye, and she grimaced at him.

"Oh, all right. I was just getting to it. I'm sorry too, Fulke. I'd no right to abuse you as I did. Though I do think that carrying a grudge is more than unbecoming in a Council member," she retorted.

Fulke swelled alarmingly and opened his mouth, but Master Eschar beat him to speaking.

"Enough. Merovice, if that is the best you can do, then it will have to serve. Fulke, there is no sense delaying further. May I suggest you begin removal of that unpleasant curse?"

The Weather Master deflated. "I can't. I—er—don't have the materials."

"Nonsense. We have everything you might need here," Eschar said.

"I didn't bring my familiar." He glared malevolently at Pol, who yawned ostentatiously and removed himself from Aunt Merry's lap to mince along the back of the sofa. "That cat—"

"You don't need your familiar with you for this," Eschar said calmly. "You didn't have him when you cast the spell. Fulke? Why don't you try telling the truth? It would save us time."

"I—I—" The little pig eyes darted desperately into every corner of the room. "I don't know what you mean."

Eschar shook his head. "Why don't you just admit that you don't want to remove the spell because you *can't?* You don't know how."

"What?" Merovice bounced up on the sofa cushion. Jermyn felt his jaw drop in dismay. "William, what are you saying?"

"He can't remove the curse because it isn't entirely his casting," Eschar explained matter-of-factly. "The one he cast, you could have solved and removed in a matter of days, probably. The one you are bearing does what Fulke wanted it to do, but it has been made more complex—has been altered—by Jermyn's interference."

"Me?" Jermyn squeaked. Delia lifted her head in sudden alarm, then apparently deciding there was no threat in the room, she went back to contemplating a plate of chocolate biscuits. "What did I do?"

"Blocked the curse with your own newly awakened talent," Eschar said. "Added a layer to the spell which Fulke didn't understand and which he was too embarrassed to ask for help in solving. Don't look so guilty, Jermyn—you hadn't the slightest idea of what you were doing. No spellmaker does, at first."

Jermyn felt his stomach turn over. "A spell-maker—me?"

Fulke turned purple. "That's ridiculous. He can't be."

"Why not?" Merovice said, positively glowing with pride. "You old fool, didn't you know your spell had been altered? If you'd admitted it, we'd have untangled this mess weeks ago."

"Congratulations, Jermyn," Inspector Andrews said, shaking his hand.

"But—but I—" He felt numb, confused—not the least like an earth wizard should feel.

"Think about it, Jermyn," Eschar said, mildness itself. "How else could you have responded instinctively to an unknown spell?"

"Aunt Merry said that when a wizard attaches a familiar, it releases a surge of power," Jermyn answered slowly.

"No doubt that is part of what did happen, with Fulke. I was thinking of the plague matrix."

"So was I," Andrews said, unexpectedly. "I've been wondering all along how Jermyn managed to deflect that spell. Even I felt it, and I'm no wizard. Journeyman Quail went down like a rock thrown off a tall building."

"That's not surprising," Fulke blustered. "Journeymen! Couldn't duck a spell-matrix if they had three days' warning."

"If you say so," Andrews responded, politely not pointing out that the Weather Master hadn't fared any better. Then he grinned, as if suddenly remembering something. "Speaking of Quail, he's a very surprised and sorry journeyman these days. Apparently getting trapped by the fear matrix taught him not to be so filled with his own significance."

"Which is all to the good," Eschar commented. "Journeyman Quail had also better work on thinking before he speaks—if he ever wants to make master."

"I wouldn't know about that," Andrews said, returning to the subject at hand. "But he *is* a journeyman now, while Jermyn is only an apprentice. However, if Jermyn is an apprentice spellmaker—well, that explains a great deal."

"But not everything," Eschar said, his voice amused. "Jermyn? Would you care to comment?"

"It was Delia," he said. The statement earned him puzzled looks from everyone but Master Eschar. "The plague matrix was triggered by fear, remember? When the person Meggan had set it into became afraid, the spell would activate. The fear would increase magically until the plague took hold."

Merovice shuddered. "I remember that bit. But how is it you weren't afraid, Jerry? You're a brave boy, but—"

"I was afraid, all right," he said, looking at Master Eschar. The Theoretician only smiled. "But Delia wasn't, because skunks don't really fear much of anything. Even when they should, sometimes. I just tapped into the familiar-bond, without even realizing what I was doing, and the spell-matrix sort of— bounced off."

Fulke snorted. "Well, so that idiot beast is good for something."

Merovice bristled. "That idiot beast saved your life, you old blowhard. If Jermyn hadn't been able to draw the girl's sting, we all might still be comatose, waiting for someone to solve the spell. How many of us would have been left alive by the time that happened? You might say thank you."

Fulke looked down. "I *am* thankful," he muttered. "I apologized, didn't I? For everything. And I meant it."

He sounded so ashamed and embarrassed that Jermyn couldn't help but believe him. Even Merovice was touched.

"Well, and I'm thankful and sorry, too," she said after a brief pause. She looked at Jermyn. "Truly. I'm thankful to Jermyn and his familiar, and sorry that I ever quarreled with you, Fulke."

There was real regret and contrition in her voice. Fulke brightened, and Jermyn smiled at her gratefully.

Master Eschar stood up. "That's better, both of you. Well done. But Fulke is going to have to do rather more than say thank you, I'm afraid. Jermyn, if you would just go stand next to him, please—"

"Are you sure, Master?" he said worriedly. "What if the focus gets away from me again?"

"It won't," the Theoretician assured him. "You were well on your way to true control before the crisis, and I believe you have achieved it now. Witness your actions at the Guild Hall on the night of the fire, and later, when you helped your aunt. All you have to do is concentrate on yourself, *inside*. Don't reach out at all. Fulke will handle the technical work. Weather Master?"

"All right, all right," Fulke said irritably, his brief good humor evaporating. He heaved himself out of his chair. "I said I would. Just don't get in my way, boy. Is that beast of yours still in the room?"

Delia had gone around behind the couch and was crouched just inside the edge of the tablecloth. Jermyn decided not to mention it.

"Yes, of course," he said. "Pol is, too. Do you need him?"

"The curse is on Merovice, not her cat," the Weather Master snapped. "Just make sure both familiars are nearby."

He clasped both hands in front of him, and began to intone the words of the spell backwards. The Theoretician leaned forward, an expression of keen interest on his face. No doubt he appreciated watching a practicing wizard at work. Inspector Andrews poured himself another cup of tea.

Merovice sat very still on the sofa, her hands in

her lap. She looked tense, but her head was up and her eyes were clear. Moved by an impulse he didn't quite understand, Jermyn lifted his left hand and held it, palm down, over Fulke's joined hands.

"That's it, Jermyn," Eschar said quietly. "Just hold it steady now."

Jermyn closed his eyes. A small cloud of darkness formed under his hand, like a miniature rain cloud. It smelled rancid, like old butter left too long in the sun. The power building up made his hand tingle, sent shivers racing up his arm.

Je'm'n? Delia asked, puzzled. *All right?*

The gold cord between them was shining softly. *Fine, Dee. Everything's fine—*

Opening his hands, Fulke flipped the palms upward as if he were throwing something away. The cloud caught against Jermyn's hand and hissed slightly, as if burning, but there was no pain. Then it dissipated, as if the sun had melted through the rain. Jermyn blinked; there was a brief arch of colors across the back of his hand, like a small rainbow, but then that too was gone, almost before he could be sure he'd really seen it.

"There," Fulke growled, stalking back to his chair. "It's done."

"Merovice?" Master Eschar said urgently. "How do you feel?"

She closed her eyes, and held very still. Jermyn

knew what she was doing: checking the link with Pol, feeling the magic flow smoothly into her.

She opened her eyes, and smiled like the sun coming up. "Very well, William. Everything's back to normal. Well done, Jermyn. Thank you."

Fulke snorted, but wisely kept his mouth shut.

Jermyn sat down heavily. He felt tired, and rather frightened. *A spellmaker. Me. Now what do I do?*

"Jermyn?" Aunt Merry said again, questioningly. "Why so dark, lad? Be happy."

"I am. Only . . ." He hesitated. "Does this mean I'll have to—to leave Master Eschar and apprentice to a spellmaker?"

"I don't believe so," the Theoretician said gravely. "I think you will do quite well with me for your apprenticeship. Lady Jean is retired, and theoreticians and spellmakers both must concern themselves with the laws and principles of magic. When you are older and more experienced, you will of course have to study with her. She will come out of retirement for that. I will make certain of it. For now, though, we can go on as we have been."

A weight lifted from Jermyn's shoulders. "Good," he said, smiling shyly at Merovice, who positively beamed at him. "I'd like that."

"And so all's well that ends well," she said, clapping her hands lightly. "Jermyn has a master who can train him in his own brave field, and Pol and I are linked again. Pol? Pol, where are you? Come out, my pretty boy. I can feel how happy you are to be with me again—"

Jermyn craned his neck. "He's right under the table over—"

There was a sudden crash from the table, just behind Fulke's chair. The weather wizard gargled in annoyance and caught at the tablecloth to steady himself as his chair started to tilt, but it was no use. He went flying, and so did most of the tablecloth, sliding onto the floor around him with a crash of breaking dishes.

In back of him, revealed by the falling chair, were Delia and Pol. The cat was crouched at the edge of the carpet, facing away from the center of the room, and Delia was just behind him. Darting forward from under the chair she had overset, she seized the tip of a yellow tail in her teeth and bit down, hard. Pol went straight up in the air, leaving behind the baked salmon that he had filched, platter and all. He made the top of the curtain in two leaps and clung there, yowling in counterpoint to Fulke's yells.

"Pol! Bad cat!" Aunt Merry cried, bouncing energetically to her feet. "You come down from there and say you're sorry."

Pol hissed savagely. Delia, bending over the abandoned salmon, looked up long enough to twitch her tail at him.

"Dee! No!" Jermyn said, grabbing for her. "Don't you dare spray."

She dug her feet in, mouth full of fish, and refused to move.

Not in the house, Je'm'n, she said to him reprovingly.

Helplessly, he looked around the room—at Fulke sputtering into the tablecloth, at Mrs. Dundee in the doorway staring openmouthed at the wreckage. Inspector Andrews was also staring openmouthed, but his face was red with suppressed laughter, while Aunt Merry was concentrating on trying to coax an outraged Pol down from the curtain.

Jermyn caught Master Eschar's eye.

"I'm sorry, sir," he said, but he wasn't, very. It felt so good to be in the middle of an ordinary mess. Delia's pointed face smiled up at him unrepentantly; she knew he wasn't really angry.

The Theoretician chuckled. "Once again I see that this is going to be a most interesting apprenticeship," he said ruefully.

From her place by the curtain, Merovice made a face at him.

"Serves you right," she said.